ALIEN ENCYCLOPEDIA

>>>

ALIEN ENCYCLOPEDIA
The Ultimate A-Z

ANDREW DONKIN

ILLUSTRATED BY PAUL FISHER-JOHNSON

Collins
VOYAGER

An imprint of HarperCollinsPublishers

First published in Great Britain by Element Children's Books 1999
Revised and updated edition published by CollinsVoyager 2002
CollinsVoyager is an imprint of HarperCollins*Publishers* Ltd
77-85 Fulham Palace Road, Hammersmith,
London, W6 8JB

The HarperCollins website address is:
www.**fire**and**water**.com

1 3 5 7 9 8 6 4 2

Text © Andrew Donkin 1999, 2002
Illustrations by Paul Fisher-Johnson 1999, 2002

ISBN 0 00 713288 3

Andrew Donkin and Paul Fisher-Johnson assert the moral right to be identified
as the author and the illustrator of the work.

Printed and bound in England by
Clays Ltd, St Ives plc

ACKNOWLEDGEMENTS

Captain's Log Supplemental – My grateful thanks to all those cosmic correspondents who trawled through their memories to fill in the missing details of the strange alien worlds and weird extraterrestrial life forms that make up this guide. Especially to:

Mr Mike Fillis, a true time-travelling gentleman who proved to be an absolute minefield of information whenever asked.

Lorne Mason, for once more opening his overflowing X-Files, and particularly for the fab Jellyfish seen in Japan.

Uncle Ronnie Fogelman and little Miss Talia Fogelman who insisted, "the Rancor is a monster not an alien" – it's under 'alien monsters', OK?

Lee Sullivan (the man I still call "El Supremo") for voyaging deep into the Skrull Empire and risking the wrath of Galactus to file reports no other human could have lived to speak of.

Paul MacGechan for supplying footage of the antics of animated aliens.

Lottie and Caroline Rauch, who know more about the sinister alien hybrids called Teletubbies than anyone should.

Stella "Ritchie Rich" Paskins for braving the sands of Dune and for being the first to pass the GAT and get a Galactic Passport.

And all those who helped along the way and those who contributed their lists of top ten aliens, not least: Sheila Brand, Olivia, Camille and Chiara Chevallier, Emma Chippendale, the original Alienmeister Barry Cunningham, Peter Donkin, Amy Finegan, little Rowan Finch, Leon Grace, Sophie Hicks, Robin Jarvis, Bernie Jaye, Janet Jenvey and Fritzi, Jane Jenvey, Dannie Kreeger, Jeff Lobel, Helen Lloyd, Don and Leslie Mason, GodMa Mandy Pink, Young Miss Julia Posen and Geoff Prout.

And lastly to Paul Fisher-Johnson for his excellent pictures and indubitably good taste.

* *

NAM ET IPSA SCIENTIA POTESTAS EST
KNOWLEDGE ITSELF IS POWER

Francis Bacon

* *

CONTENTS

>>>

THE UNIVERSE TODAY

The universe today is a large and dangerous place. Unwitting travellers can find themselves exterminated, imprisoned, or become a light afternoon snack for hungry, flesh-eating monsters before they can scream, "Two cheap day returns to Sirius, please." And that is where this book comes in. The Alien Encyclopedia is designed to help you stay alive.

This book is aimed at both the casual space tourist and the more serious and hardened galactic traveller. From those heading for the sunbeds of Tatooine on a cut-price package deal, to those backpacking around the uncharted galactic rim and beyond.

With more and more alien worlds joining the interstellar community every zarb*, it's getting harder and harder to keep track of who is who, and which blue and yellow tentacled thing is which blue and yellow tentacled thing.

The following statistics speak volumes. Of those humans already holidaying on alien planets:

- 30% of those asked said that they felt they would have got more from their holiday if they had known more about the culture and customs of their alien hosts;

* equal to about ten Earth days – see you're learning things already!

- 22% found that language difficulties made it impossible for them to complain about the state of their hotel rooms when they wanted to;

- And 15% had a member of the family eaten alive while on holiday.

For the space traveller today the three main problems of life out in the big wide cosmos are the same as they have always been:

1/ How do I avoid accidentally giving offence to my alien host and causing a galactic war?

2/ Is that multi-jawed alien waiter with drool running down his face thinking of serving me or eating me?

3/ Where can I possibly get reasonably priced toilet paper on Vulcan after midnight when the shops have shut?

This volume attempts to answer all of those questions and many more you didn't even know you wanted to ask.

>>>

HOW TO USE THIS BOOK

First-time space travellers should work their way through this book in order, making detailed notes and eating them twice a day.

We begin with a look at Earthbound alien research in 'Evidence', and then move on to cover the alarming number of would-be invaders of Earth in 'Conspiracies'. 'Tourists and Explorers' covers aliens likely to be encountered without even having to leave Earth, while 'Shapeshifters' details those sneaky alien species able to disguise themselves as other people.

It's not all bad news though, and 'Allies' lists the races very likely to offer you a cup of tea and a slice of cake while journeying in the great beyond. Then it's back to facts that'll keep you alive as we cover 'Enemies and Aggressors', 'Oddballs', 'Alien Kidnappers' and finally the alarming and entirely fearful, sweat-inducing 'Monsters and Creatures'.

For the brave explorers who are not put off leaving their living room, the end of the book features the Galactic Aptitude Test (GAT). Would-be cosmic voyagers from Earth must pass this to earn their Galactic Passport.

ALIEN EVIDENCE

The human species has always looked skywards with wonder. Today, most of the attention and interest is directed not at the stars and planets themselves, but rather at the possibility that some of them might be teeming with alien life forms.

Some human beings claim to have met aliens without ever having left their native planet. This first data file examines the state of Earthbound UFOlogy – the study of UFOs and alien encounters. How much do the planet's top alien hunters think they know about life beyond Earth…?

>>>

ABDUCTORS

ABDUCTIONS

WHAT ARE THEY? Some humans claim to have experienced alien contact without ever having left Earth. According to the many witnesses, abductions by visiting aliens are on the increase. Barney and Betty Hill's encounter on 19 September 1961 is a textbook case of what the abductee can expect.

APPEARANCE: The Hills' description of their abductors was one of the first reports of the alien type that would later become known as the Grey. Just over one metre tall, the aliens had large heads, big, dark eyes and just a thin slit for a mouth. Most of the creatures were dressed in identical uniforms.

MISSION: Abduction for medical tests.

PLANET OF ORIGIN: The aliens showed Betty a 'star map' which a UFO researcher later suggested was of the star system Zeta Reticulii – although this theory has been much disputed.

ENCOUNTERED WHEN? The Hills were driving home from a holiday late at night when they spotted a bright, star-like object following them in the sky. The object moved in front of their car and Barney saw that it was a spacecraft full of small, humanoid creatures. The couple fled in terror. When they arrived home, they found it was two hours later than it should have been – a classic case of missing time.

AFTER-EFFECTS: Suffering from strange nightmares, the couple agreed to be hypnotised. Under hypnosis they remembered being taken on board the aliens' craft and being examined by the curious creatures.

This case was turned into a book – *The Interrupted Journey* by journalist John G Fuller. It was the first alien abduction case to receive widespread publicity.

BLOODLINES

WHAT ARE THEY? Some UFO investigators believe that alien abduction often happens down generations of the same family. They suggest that the aliens may be keeping tabs on specific cases over decades, monitoring any genetic changes in their subjects' offspring.

* *

CLOSE ENCOUNTERS

WHAT ARE THEY? Contact between human and alien life forms. Betty Andreasson witnessed the following example on 25 January 1967 at her home in Massachusetts, USA.

APPEARANCE: Two different species were involved in this encounter and abduction. One type was small with large, dark eyes and big, domed heads. The second type was smaller still, with three-fingered hands, two arms and legs, but no head. Where the neck should have been there were two large eyes on long stalks.

MISSION: Culture swap and abduction.

PLANET OF ORIGIN: Ms Andreasson was told the name of their home world began with the letter Z, but humans would find it unpronounceable.

ENCOUNTERED WHEN? Betty noticed a strange, orange light coming in the kitchen window. Before she could react, five beings walked into the kitchen through the wall.

Under hypnosis years later, Betty recalled meeting the aliens' leader who said his name was Quazga. They took Betty on board their saucer-shaped spacecraft and examined her using a variety of different medical probes. **>>>**

CLOSE ENCOUNTERS

After this, they emerged into a planet or dimension with a red atmosphere and it was here that she saw the creatures with eyes on stalks, climbing buildings as if they were monkeys.

ALIEN ADVICE: The leader gave Betty a thin book containing their religious teachings, but she lost it before she got home. She was also given a message of peace to bring to the people of Earth.

AFTER-EFFECTS: Betty also remembered other earlier abductions by the same species of alien. The entire case history is detailed in the book *The Andreasson Affair* by Raymond Fowler.

* *

ANDREW COLLINS

OCCUPATION: Author and researcher based in England.

CAREER: Andrew Collins has made a study of different elements of the paranormal for over two decades. He began his career as a UFO investigator, before becoming interested in more literally down-to-earth matters such as ancient sites, ley lines and crop circles. He became a leading figure in the questing movement, before setting his intellect to work on the mysteries of Ancient Egypt and the location of Atlantis.

MOST FAMOUS CASE: Collins was the original investigator into what became known as the 'Aveley Abduction' which took place in Aveley, Essex, England. Driving home late at night on 27 October 1974, an entire family of five was abducted by two different species of aliens working together. John and Elaine Avis and their three children spotted a bright, pale-blue light in the sky keeping pace with their car. Turning a corner in the road, John found himself driving into a bank of thick, green mist and the car engine went dead.

 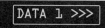

The next thing they remembered was a jolt, and the family was driving along again. However, when they reached home, they were puzzled to find that it was three hours later than it should have been.

WHAT HAPPENED NEXT? After months of disturbing dreams, John Avis sought advice from a UFO research group and was eventually contacted by Andrew Collins.

Under hypnotic regression, John recalled their car being taken on board a large craft. Inside were tall, wise-looking aliens he dubbed 'Watchers' as well as shorter, hairy aliens with claws for hands, wearing white doctors' coats. John was shown a 3-D holographic image of a devastated Earth and given a warning about pollution and the future of the planet.

John's wife Elaine recalled exactly the same events when she underwent hypnosis. Their matching stories make the Avis case one of Britain's best-documented encounters with aliens.

* *

CRASH WRECKAGE

WHAT IS IT? In recent decades there have been several stories of alien spacecraft that have crashed on Earth, their wreckage and the remains of alien bodies supposedly being taken away by government authorities.

MOST FAMOUS CASE: The granddaddy of all crash wreckage stories is the case which occurred in the summer of 1947 at Roswell, New Mexico, USA. William Brazel was riding across his ranch when he chanced upon the wreckage of something that had crashed out of the sky the night before.

The military soon moved in to claim the pieces of wreckage for themselves. Major Jesse Marcel issued an extraordinary press >>>

statement saying that the crash debris was the remains of a flying saucer, but almost immediately seemed to change his mind and made another statement claiming that it had been a weather balloon.

WAS IT A SPACECRAFT? Some UFO investigators believe that the wreckage was from an extraterrestrial ship and that the remains were taken and stored at the Wright Patterson Air Base. Since then, they believe the wreckage has been the subject of study by scientists trying to unlock its technological secrets.

Although there is no reliable evidence, some believe that actual alien bodies were recovered from the site. Rumours and unconfirmed film footage hint that the bodies may have been the subject of an autopsy before being frozen in ice.

* *

CROP CIRCLES

WHAT ARE THEY? Artificial patterns formed in farmers' fields. Crop circles vary in size and their designs can be anything from simple circles to gigantic, complex formations. The modern era of the crop circle began in the late 1970s in Hampshire and Wiltshire in England.

The new formations seem to become more complex with each passing 'season'. Recent years have seen the formation of patterns based on advanced mathematical formulae. Researchers working in the field are called Cerealogists. Similar designs imprinted into sand, snow and grass have been spotted in many countries around the world.

HOW ARE THEY FORMED? There are several theories:

- They are messages from a superior intelligence – either the occupants of alien spacecraft, or somehow the Earth itself speaking to humans.

- They are caused by unknown but natural atmospheric conditions, including stationary whirlwinds and plasma vortices. The problem with this theory is that many crop circles seem much too complex to be the work of random whirlwinds.

- They are made by human hoaxers working secretly at night for their own amusement. While some circles are undoubtedly the work of pranksters, many others remain unexplained.

- They are the result of ball lightning or Earth energies moving over the field. Several witnesses have seen spheres of light moving over fields moments before a formation has appeared.

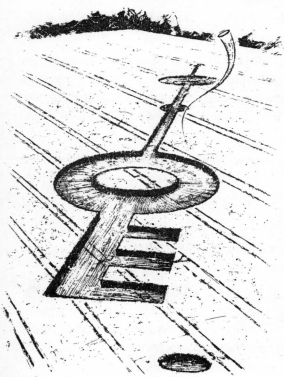

WHEN DO THEY OCCUR? Usually overnight – when no one's looking.

HISTORY: Records of crop circles have been found centuries before the modern outbreak. As long ago as 1590, strange patterns in fields were noted by farmers and entered local folklore in England as the work of 'mowing devils'.

FACE ON MARS

WHAT IS IT? In the summer of 1976, the unmanned NASA probes *Viking I* and *Viking II* reached Mars's orbit and took more than 60,000 pictures of the planet's surface. Apart from providing detailed images of the previously uncharted terrain, a few of the pictures appeared to show a rock formation in the shape of a giant face.

WHERE IS IT? The Face is in a part of Mars called the Cydonia Mensae region. It has been suggested that scattered around the Face are other artificial structures including pyramids. The Face on Mars led some researchers to believe they had at last found evidence of life on other worlds.

ARTIFICIAL OR A TRICK OF THE LIGHT? Another set of pictures taken more recently by another NASA probe seemed to show that the Face was just a trick of the light. Some researchers, however, suspect that the new pictures were faked by NASA. The final verdict will have to wait for more evidence.

* *

FRAUDS

WHAT ARE THEY? Occasionally, the UFO investigator comes across a case where the witness has deliberately made up their story for their own purpose. Consider the curious case of the Swedish Space Slugs.

WHAT HAPPENED? On 20 December 1958, Hans Gustafsson and Stig Rydberg claimed they had seen a disc-shaped object descend from the sky and that when they went to investigate, they were attacked by metre-high grey slugs who tried to pull them towards the ship.

AFTER-EFFECTS: The case became quite famous in their native Sweden and the men soon began making money on the lecture circuit describing their experiences. Although many UFO investigators were quick to believe them at the time, their story was completely made up, a fact they later confessed to friends and family.

* *

GREYS

WHO ARE THEY? Greys are the most commonly seen and reported species of alien to visit Earth. The Grey and variations of the Grey account for many of the most famous UFO/abduction cases on record.

WHY ARE THEY SO COMMON? There are three main theories:

1/ The variations of the Grey seen are in fact one species reported differently by panicked witnesses.

2/ They are different species from different worlds who have evolved along similar lines, in the same way that humans, Vulcans, Time Lords and Minbari are all broadly similar humanoids

3/ They are entities not of this universe at all, who are here to help 'recycle souls'.

HOAXES

WHAT ARE THEY? Whereas frauds are usually perpetrated for personal gain, hoaxes, more often than not, poke fun at the subject they are hoaxing.

EXAMPLE: In the 1960s a number of farmers across southern England received a shock one morning when they found a series of small flying saucers had landed in their fields. The bleeping craft were a prank and had been left overnight by students as part of their university rag week activities. The line of saucers stretched from Somerset in the west, all the way to Kent.

 H > I

 DATA 1 >>>

BUDD HOPKINS

OCCUPATION: UFO investigator based in New York City, USA.

CAREER: Budd Hopkins is a talented painter and sculptor whose work has been shown in galleries and museums all over America. He became interested in the phenomenon of alien abduction and began to investigate the subject seriously in the early 1980s.

Since then, Hopkins has become a leading authority on the subject and published many books detailing his findings. It was Hopkins who helped author Whitley Strieber 'recover' his own alien memories, which became the best-selling book *Communion*. Hopkins has investigated more than 1500 separate cases and is still out there seeking the truth.

WORKS: *Missing Time*, a study of seven abduction accounts, was one of the first books to feature abductions exclusively. *Intruders* details the now famous Kathie Davis/Copley Woods case, one of the longest-running abduction cases on record.

STRENGTHS: Hopkins is a careful investigator, gathering as many facts as he can and allowing his readers to weigh up the evidence for themselves.

* *

IMPLANTS

WHAT ARE THEY? Many of the alien visitors to Earth are rumoured to use implants to assist in their study of humankind. The implants are placed inside the body of the human subject during the abduction process. The nasal cavity and the back of the neck seem to be the favourite hiding places.

WHAT ARE THEY FOR? Possibly tracking devices which allow the aliens to pinpoint the subject's location for the next abduction. >>>

CLASSIFIED DATA: Recognising that an implant of provable alien origin would be hard evidence of their existence, there have been several attempts by UFO investigators to recover these objects from witnesses using surgical procedures. Although some objects have been removed, none so far has been of clearly alien manufacture.

FAMOUS CASE: It was suggested that Gulf Breeze witness Ed Walters (see page 204) had an implant in his head, but this could be investigated, he was abducted again and the device was removed by its alien owners.

* *

JOHN MACK

OCCUPATION: Harvard-educated psychiatrist, author of *Abduction: Human Encounters with Aliens*.

CAREER: Mack caused major controversy with his book about alien abductions and creatures 'from beyond the veil'. Most arguments centred on the fact that a top academic and Pulitzer Prize winner like Mack should have taken the subject so seriously, let alone support his patients' belief that their experiences were real. In recent works, Mack argues that aliens come not from another planet but from another reality – a kind of parallel universe. He claims the entities are trying to make humans understand the cosmic realities that exist beyond their three-dimensional universe.

* *

MAJESTIC 12

WHAT IS IT? Supposedly, a top secret group of scientists, military personnel and secret service agents which was set up following the recovery of the Roswell saucer in 1947.

The truth about the existence of Majestic 12 has long been the subject of fierce debate within UFO circles. Documents relating to the group's members and activities have appeared on the Internet, but some suspect hoaxers of faking them. Others suggest that the CIA may be using today's UFO investigators to spread misinformation.

* *

LORNE MASON

OCCUPATION: Researcher and paranormal investigator.

CAREER: Lorne R Mason has been gathering UFO reports and information on alien abductions for over two decades and has a huge database of information from cases all over the world. His job with one of Britain's leading broadcasting and communications companies gives him the opportunity to talk to witnesses and gather on-site data all over the world.

MASON

MEN IN BLACK (MIBs)

WHO ARE THEY? Sinister men dressed in dark suits who visit witnesses to UFO sightings in an effort to compel them to remain silent about what they have seen. The MIB often issue vague threats to witnesses, but never seem to carry them out.

They were a more common feature of the UFO scene in the 1960s and 1970s than today, although the occasional MIB visit still takes place. It is a matter of speculation whether they are government agents trying to continue the UFO cover-up, or agents of the aliens themselves.

* *

MISSING TIME

WHAT IS IT? Missing time is one of the most common features of alien abduction reports. Typically, witnesses remember little or nothing of their alien encounter beyond a distant light in the sky or an approaching UFO. However, when finishing their journey they realise that it is later than they had expected and that a period of time has elapsed of which they have no memory. It is often under just these circumstances that witnesses volunteer to undergo hypnotic regression in an effort to fill in the blanks.

* *

NICK POPE

OCCUPATION: Former civil servant turned author.

CAREER: Pope worked for the British Ministry of Defence as a higher executive officer. For three years he was appointed to Secretariat (Air Staff) Department 2A – known to government insiders as the UFO Desk.

As time went on and Pope investigated more and more UFO cases, he became convinced that the reports were real and that the Earth was being visited regularly by extraterrestrial spacecraft. He put his thoughts on paper in his books *Open Skies, Closed Minds* and *The Uninvited*.

* *

PROJECT BLUE BOOK

WHAT WAS IT? Created in 1952, Project Blue Book was the US Air Force's official investigation of UFOs. The project was commanded by Captain Edward Ruppelt and based at Wright Patterson Air Base. It was closed down in 1969.

WHAT DID IT DO? Its staff interviewed UFO witnesses all over the country, reporting back on each individual case. During its years of operation, Blue Book investigated 12,618 reports of strange objects in the skies over America. Many observers believed that Project Blue Book was an attempt to sweep the UFO phenomenon under the carpet.

FAMOUS FACE: Project Blue Book's scientific adviser for many years was renowned scientist Dr J Allen Hynek, a professor of astronomy. He continued to be a major force in UFO research up until his death in 1986.

* *

JENNY RANDLES

OCCUPATION: One of Britain's leading alien researchers and authors.

CAREER: Actively involved in UFO research since the 1960s and has written countless books on all aspects of the UFO and alien field, including *Abduction, Star Children* and *The Paranormal Source Book*.

SETI

WHAT DOES IT STAND FOR? Search for Extraterrestrial Intelligence.

WHAT IS IT? Big budget programme to search for intelligent messages from alien life forms across the galaxy. There are currently 25 other separate projects under the SETI umbrella including investigations of exobiology, Mars and planetary science.

MOST FAMOUS FOR? Project Phoenix, which uses the largest radio telescopes in the world to listen for signals from nearby sun-like stars. It searches for signals in the 1000 MHz to 3000 MHz range believing that's where any intelligent ETs would probably be broadcasting. Project Phoenix costs $5 million per year to run, a figure met entirely by voluntary contributions.

SETI scientists believe that there is intelligent life out there in the universe, but are dismissive of the notion that aliens may be visiting Earth already.

TUNGUSKA EXPLOSION

WHAT WAS IT? An enormous, airborne explosion that occurred over Siberia on 30 June 1908. Locals reported seeing a bright, gleaming object travelling very quickly through the sky towards the forests of Tunguska.

WHAT CAUSED IT? A meteorite or small comet remain the most likely candidates for what created the miles and miles of devastation that morning, but some investigators believe that an extraterrestrial craft attempting a crash landing could have been the cause. Another theory is that the huge explosion was caused by a small fragment of antimatter striking the planet.

* *

JACQUES VALLEE

OCCUPATION: Writer and researcher.

CAREER: Dr Vallee was born in France and trained as an astrophysicist. He became interested in UFOs when he witnessed tracking tapes of unknown objects being deliberately destroyed at a major observatory.

His approach to the subject linked UFOs with the fairy phenomenon of past centuries and speculated that the aliens might be from another dimension altogether. He has published many books and is one of the leading authorities on UFOs and alien encounters in the world.

MOST LIKELY TO SAY: "Although I am among those who believe that UFOs are real, physical objects, I do not think they are extraterrestrial in the ordinary sense of the term. In my view, they prsent an exciting challenge to our concept of reality itself... If these objects have been seen from time immemorial... perhaps they have always been here. On Earth. With us."

VISITORS

VISITORS

WHO ARE THEY? Small, humanoid aliens that regularly visit the author Whitley Strieber. Strieber believes that his encounters with these beings began during his childhood and have continued through much of his adult life until today.

APPEARANCE: The Visitors are a variation of the traditional Grey (see page 21). About one metre tall, they have high cheekbones and very large, dark eyes. Close up, they have been reported as having a musty, woodsy smell.

PLANET OF ORIGIN: Unknown, but possibly from another dimension or plane of existence.

ENCOUNTERED WHEN? Strieber had a series of frightening, late-night encounters with the Visitors while staying at his isolated country cabin in the woods.

At first Strieber was forcibly abducted against his will. The creatures dragged him out of the cabin and into the dark night. When he complained that they had no right to do that, they assured him in a low voice: "We have a right."

They kept returning and gradually he learned to control his fear, believing that they were adding to his inner development.

THE OWL CONNECTION: Strieber's Visitors seem connected to owls. The nocturnal birds often appear beforehand or even turn into Visitors. The owls are not what they seem.

ALIEN ADVICE: Strieber's aliens are described as 'agents of change' helping humankind evolve, perhaps even to survive.

>>>

AFTER-EFFECTS: Strieber's first book, *Communion*, stayed in the bestseller charts for months and he has produced several follow-ups. His huge success reawakened public interest in alien abductions in the late 1980s. His other works include: *Transformation, Breakthrough, The Communion Letters* and *The Secret School*.

DATA 1 COMPLETE

ALIEN CONSPIRACIES

Inhabitable worlds with a supply of abundant water, an oxygen-rich atmosphere, pleasant temperatures and a good dry-cleaning service are few and far between in the universe. Earth has long been considered a 'blue-green jewel' of a planet ripe for conquest.

From Pod People who hatch looking like your next-door neighbours, to the cunning plan of the Midwich Cuckoos, this data file examines just some of the races itching to get their tentacles on your home world...

>>>

COLONISTS

ORGANISATION: The Conspiracy.

SPECIES: Combination of humans and aliens working together.

APPEARANCE: Men in dark suits and alien shapeshifters.

WHO ARE THEY? These are the guys who always get away from Mulder and Scully. According to the long-deceased Deep Throat they include, "black organisations, groups within groups, conducting covert activities unknown at the highest levels of power". They're also aliens hoping to eventually turn Earth into a colony, i.e. take over the planet.

STRENGTHS: No one understands what's really, really going on. Not Mulder. Not Scully. Not Doggett. Probably not even the guys doing it. As Scully has said, "It's kind of hard to tell the villains without a scorecard."

WEAKNESSES: See Strengths.

TACTICS: The Conspiracy has known about the existence of aliens since World War II and has had samples of alien DNA since the Roswell crash of 1947.

THE SHAPESHIFTERS: Immensely strong and physically powerful, the shapeshifting assassins have been used to kill those who know too much and those who misuse the aliens' technology. Fellow shapeshifters can recognise each other no matter whose face they're wearing and they can heal human wounds and injuries when they want to.

Shapeshifters can be killed only by a deep incision at the back of the neck. Their blood is green and poisonous to humans. There is a group of rebel shapeshifters fighting against the efforts of the others.

MOST LIKELY TO SAY: "Deny everything."

THE DOG EMPIRE

WHO ARE THEY? Rumours continue to circulate around the galactic core that humankind has fallen victim to one of the most cunning and well-concealed alien takeovers of all time. Dogs – highly intelligent aliens with strong telepathic powers – are said to have conquered Earth thousands of years ago turning it into an outpost of the Dog Empire.

WHAT HAPPENED? According to secret Dog history, Dogs arrived some time around 100,000 BC and set about educating and evolving human-kind's primitive ancestors to a level where they could form communities and care for their new masters (i.e. Dogs).

LIFESTYLE: Dogs all over the world now live in extreme comfort, having their meals prepared and their every need taken care of by their human subjects.

WHO'S IN CHARGE? The secret Dog Empire appoints a Pack Leader on each planet. In control of its Earth branch are rumoured to be two miniature dachshunds: Pack Leader Scooby and her assistant Fritzi.

The Dog Emperor frequently picks the smallest Dog on each world to rule – a clever double bluff in case of alien attack.

ENEMIES: Have been locked in a long-running war with an alien species known as Cats for thousands of years. Most planets in the inhabited universe have been the battleground for this secret, galactic tussle.

At the last count, Dogs ruled 314 worlds, Cats 296, with the conflict still undecided on another 378,201,204,382,956,012,925 planets.

* *

THE INVADERS

WHO WERE THEY? A race of aliens from a dying planet who tried to infiltrate all levels of Earth society in an effort to quietly gain control of the planet.

ENEMIES: They were opposed by just one man – American architect David Vincent, who had the misfortune to stumble across a flying saucer after getting lost while driving home from a business trip.

WEAKNESSES: The Invaders needed to regularly recharge themselves in order to maintain their human form. Their little finger on each hand always stuck out at a strange angle.

* *

THE MIDWICH CUCKOOS

WHAT WERE THEY? The result of a clever and devious attempt to take over the Earth by using human women to carry the seeds of their alien conquerors.

WHAT HAPPENED? After the English village of Midwich suffered a strange blackout, all the women of child-bearing age found themselves pregnant. Nine months later they gave birth to similar children, all with fair hair and unearthly, golden eyes.

>>>

The children grew up to display frightening mental powers and made no secret of their wish to inherit the planet: "Will you agree to be superseded, and start on the way to extinction without a struggle?"

They were killed in an explosion detonated by the one human they had grown to trust.

DANGER ASSESSMENT: "On the one hand, it is our duty to our race and culture to liquidate the Children, for it is clear that if we do not we shall, at best, be completely dominated by them, and their culture, whatever it may turn out to be, will extinguish ours."

* *

MULDER

NAME: Fox William Mulder.

OCCUPATION: Ex-FBI Special Agent – once attached to the X-Files.

APPEARANCE: Hunk.

DOB: 13 October 1961.

HISTORY: Mulder attended Oxford University, England, and eventually became a psychologist for the FBI. His early work, 'Serial Killers and the Occult', is still regarded as a classic paper on the subject. Mulder's first official case involved him with the capture of armed robber Johnny Barnett.

Mulder's preoccupation with aliens and the paranormal began when he was twelve and he witnessed the abduction of his eight-year-old sister Samantha. His father, Bill Mulder, was involved with the men behind the alien conspiracy. It was later discovered that Samantha was abducted to ensure his co-operation.

>>>

OFF-DUTY AGENTS

Mulder himself was abducted and went missing for several months. Finally, his apparently dead body was recovered from open countryside and he was buried. Mulder lay in his grave for over three months before Scully (see page 47) and other FBI colleagues pieced together clues that indicated that Mulder was not really dead. Like other recent abduction victims, Mulder recovered from being a seemingly lifeless corpse and was reunited with Scully.

Later, Mulder travelled to an oil rig in the Gulf of Mexico. He was intending to investigate workers there for possible infection by the Black Oil. His interference resulted in the destruction of the oil platform and finally, after many years on the edge, he was fired from the FBI. His departure left his precious X-Files in the care of Special Agent John Doggett and Special Agent Monica Reyes.

LIFESTYLE: Enjoys late-night, trashy movies and sleeping on his couch instead of the bed. Eats sunflower seeds just like his dad. Has fathered a child, William, with ex-FBI partner Scully.

STRENGTHS: Dogged determination and occasional enormous leaps of logic that defy belief, but are nearly always spot on regardless.

COMPUTER PASSWORD: trustno1

MOST LIKELY TO SAY: "I have lived with a fragile faith built on vague memories from an experience I could neither prove nor explain... What happened to me out on the ice has justified every belief. If I should die now it would be with the certainty that my faith has been righteous, and if through death larger mysteries are revealed I will have already learned the answer to the question that has driven me here: that there is intelligent life in the universe, other than our own, that they are here among us, and that they have begun to colonise."

MYSTERONS

WHO ARE THEY? Sworn enemies of Earth. As humankind explored Mars, the personnel on the mission misread the peaceful gestures of the Mysterons and opened fire on their city complex. Ever since, the Mysterons have waged a terrorist-style war on Earth. >>>

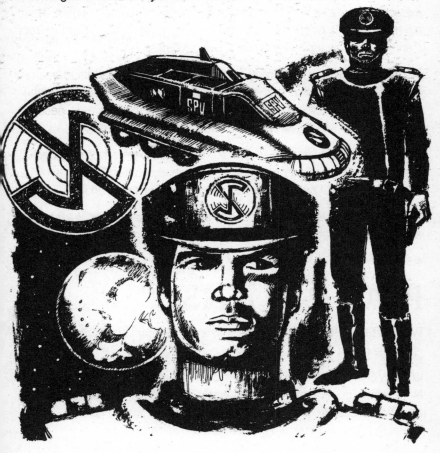

ALIEN CONSPIRACIES

Humankind is defended by the forces of Spectrum – a huge organisation with men and machines all over the world. Spectrum's home of operations is Cloudbase controlled by Colonel White.

PLANET OF ORIGIN: Mars.

STRENGTHS: They can kill or destroy, then, using the power of 'retro-metabolism' they re-form their victim who is now under their control. Their agent on Earth is Captain Black, who is opposed by Captain Scarlet. Both men are indestructible as a result of being Mysteronised.

WEAKNESSES: The Mysterons have one flaw that has held them back from being successful in their crusade: they always taunt Spectrum with a warning/riddle, telling them where they are going to strike next. As a result, they are nearly always beaten before they get started.

BATTLE TACTICS: As detailed above – their tactics were to give away their top secret plans at the beginning of each encounter. Thanks to Mysteronisation, they used the Earth's own weapons against it.

SCHEMES INCLUDED: Attempting to assassinate the World President, attempting to destroying London and later the whole of North America.

* *

PLAN 9 ALIENS

WHO WERE THEY? Eros and his partner Tanna came to Earth to put into effect their Plan 9 From Outer Space.

WHY WERE THEY HERE? To create an army of zombies to defeat humankind. Eros wanted to ensure that humans never discovered the secret of Solaronite bombs and thus endanger the entire universe. The plan failed and their ship was destroyed in an explosion.

POD PEOPLE
(AKA BODY SNATCHERS)

APPEARANCE: Exact duplicates of humans.

WHO ARE THEY? Pod People are aliens who pose as human beings, taking on their shape and form while draining the original of life. They can become your best friend, your mother or your girlfriend.

They are exact copies of humans, down to their memories, but they have no emotions or personality.

>>>

DUPLICATES

PLANET OF ORIGIN: Their original home became a barren world. They made their way to Earth by drifting through space in the form of seed pods.

BATTLE TACTICS: To quietly replace people, leading the remaining humans to feel understandably paranoid.

WEAPONS: Secrecy and stealth.

HISTORY: Instead of waging a military war like the Daleks or Borg, an invasion by the Body Snatchers is a quiet, undercover event. Reports suggest that there have been three Pod People incidents on Earth in recent times.

The first was in Santa Mira, California, in 1955. It was foiled by Dr Miles Bennell who alerted the authorities to the alien takeover.

The second happened in 1978, with yet another in the early 1990s, suggesting the drifting seed pods may continue to pose a threat for some years to come.

* *

QUATERMASS

NAME: Professor Bernard Quatermass.

OCCUPATION: Father of British rocket science. Led the British Rocket Group in the 1950s when he defeated several alien threats to Earth.

CAREER: Quatermass's first alien entanglement came after one of his earliest experimental rockets was knocked off course, travelling hundreds of thousands of kilometres away from Earth orbit. The three-man ship crashed-landed in Wimbledon but only one crew member, Victor Carroon, survived.

>>>

MARTIAN HIVE

It gradually emerged that while in space, Carroon had been infected by an alien virus of some kind that changed his body tissue into a kind of fast growing vegetation. Quatermass was on hand to save the world from the menace he had unexpectedly released.

In his second encounter with aliens, Quatermass found himself uncovering a plot to invade Earth. Creatures from an asteroid on the dark side of the Earth were sending materials to the vanguard of their race secreted in a huge domed chemical plant. Quatermass fought against their mind-control techniques and eventually defeated them.

Quatermass' next alien menace came not from the skies, but from underground. Work on a new London tube station, Hobbs Lane, had unearthed a five-million-year-old human skull together with a buried Martian spaceship. Three petrified alien insects were recovered, unleashing long forgotten forces.

FINAL CASE: After defeating the Martian menace, Quatermass retired and lived for a while as a recluse in Scotland. Decades later, and with society on the verge of total collapse, he began a search for his missing granddaughter. He found that a mysterious and unknown alien force had returned to 'harvest' the youth of the planet as they gathered in huge crowds at ancient stone circles around the world.

In a brave conclusion to a long and distinguished career, Quatermass set a trap for the alien force and detonated a nuclear bomb, sacrificing himself, but saving humanity.

MOST LIKELY TO SAY: "If another of these things should ever be found, we are armed with knowledge. But we also have knowledge of ourselves... of the ancient, destructive urges in us that grow more deadly as our populations approach in size and complexity those of ancient Mars. Every war crisis, witch hunt, race riot and purge... is a reminder and warning. We are the Martians. If we cannot control the inheritance within us... this will be their second dead planet!"

SCULLY

NAME: Dana Katherine Scully MD.

OCCUPATION: FBI Special Agent attached to the X-Files.

APPEARANCE: Red-headed goddess.

DOB: 23 February 1963.

HISTORY: Scully was recruited out of medical school by the FBI and taught at the academy at Quantico for two years. She was originally assigned to work with Mulder (see page 38) on the X-Files to keep an eye on him and possibly disprove the worth of his work.

Since then they have tackled over a hundred X-Files together. Although they developed into an extremely effective team, their cases often raised more questions than they answered.

Early in the second year of their partnership, Scully was abducted by unknown forces and given an implant in the back of her neck. Removing it caused her to develop a cancer-like illness, which only went into remission after the chip was replaced. Scully was diagnosed as unable to have children, yet recently gave birth to Mulder's son. Although seemingly human, it is quite possible that young William may have unusual abilities connected to the alien conspiracy that has obsessed his parents for so long.

HOBBIES: Carrying out autopsies, any time, any place.

MOST LIKELY TO SAY: "Many of the things I have seen have challenged my faith in an ordered universe, but this uncertainty has only strengthened my need to know, to understand, to apply reason to those things which seemed to defy it."

SHADO ALIENS

WHO WERE THEY? A species which made regular trips to Earth for spare parts and new bodies. The dying and sterile race used spinning, pyramid-shaped craft to travel the vast distance across space so they could abduct humans as either host bodies or for spare-part surgery.

ALIEN MENACE

Σ > V

DATA 2 >>>

The aliens wore bright-red spacesuits and their helmets contained a green liquid used to protect them during their spaceflight.

WHO PROTECTED EARTH? The Supreme Headquarters Alien Defence Organisation (SHADO) with an impressive collection of high-tech vehicles and spacecraft. The first line of defence was Moonbase and its interceptor craft. When UFOs did reach the Earth, they were met by Skydivers in the atmosphere and were tracked down by SHADOmobiles when they crash-landed.

The existence of the alien menace was kept from the public because governments feared a world-wide panic if the truth ever got out.

SHADO was led by Commander Straker, who, despite his best efforts, learnt very little about the aliens during the secret war.

* *

THE VISITORS
(AKA SIRIANS)

WHO WERE THEY? The Visitors' huge mother ships suddenly appeared above the major capital cities of the world. Posing as a friendly and benevolent force, they were led by the seemingly beautiful Diana. It was not long, however, before the aliens were revealed in their true form as repulsive reptiles, actually called Sirians.

MISSION: World domination and stealing Earth's water supplies.

WHO PROTECTED EARTH? A resistance movement led by Mike Donovan and Julie Parris formed to fight the Nazi-like regime. They won a battle, if not the war, with the use of a red dust that was poisonous to the Visitors.

X-FILES

ORGANISATION: Part of the FBI.

PURPOSE: To deal with criminal cases that contain elements of the paranormal, extraterrestrial or the just plain weird.

WHO ARE THEY?

Mulder: For many years the X-Files were in the charge of Special Agent Fox Mulder. 'Spooky' Mulder had a lifelong interest in UFOs and the supernatural. He has now been fired from the FBI. (See page 38.)

Scully: Special Agent Dana Scully was assigned to the X-Files in 1992, primarily to keep tabs on the maverick work of Mulder. The pair have since formed a close bond of trust and mutual respect. (See page 47.)

Doggett: Special Agent John Doggett served in the New York City Police Department before joining the FBI. He was assigned to lead the task force investigating Mulder's disappearance and became Scully's partner for several X-File cases that followed.

Since Mulder's return and sacking from the FBI, and Scully's time away from the office, he is now in nominal charge of the X-Files and works with Special Agent Monica Reyes.

KNOWN ASSOCIATES: The X-Files office answers to Assistant Director Walter S Skinner. Skinner has gone out on a limb for Mulder and Scully on many occasions.

Other likely associates include the Lone Gunmen – a group of three conspiracy-theory experts.

KNOWN ENEMIES: Many, including the manipulative insider known as the Cigarette-Smoking Man AKA Cancer Man (now believed

>>>

THE TRUTH IS OUT THERE

dead), ex-FBI Agent Alex 'Ratboy' Krycek (also believed dead), Eugene Tooms (a genetic mutant), as well as the occasional shape-changing, alien bounty hunter and alien enhanced 'super soldiers'.

ARREST RATE: While the two agents have undoubtedly had some successes, the arrest and conviction rate of the X-Files section must be one of the lowest in the entire FBI. As Mulder has said, "One of the luxuries of hunting down aliens and genetic mutants – you rarely get to press charges."

THE FUTURE: Continuing to try to uncover the vast government/alien conspiracy that has been going on for the past five decades and exposing the existence of aliens known only as the Colonists (see page 34).

DATA 2 COMPLETE

ALIEN TOURISTS AND EXPLORERS

The urge to explore the cosmos isn't just a human instinct. Across the universe, thousands of strange races and peoples are designing spaceships so that they can drop in whenever they feel like it.

The lazy galactic traveller or cosmic couch potato knows that there is often no need to go out into the great, cold vastness of space in search of alien life. Ready or not, sometimes it comes to you...

>>>

ABYSS ALIENS

WHO ARE THEY? Originating from a high-pressure water world, this species was discovered living peacefully deep down in the Earth's oceans.

TACTICS: Disturbed by the arrival of humans searching for the survivors of a submarine wreck, the aliens emerged from hiding. They demonstrated their total control over water by sending huge tidal waves towards every coast in the world and then stopping them at the last moment. The aliens demanded that humans halt their violent ways.

* *

ALF

APPEARANCE: One metre tall, covered in orange-brown hair and with a snout that would make an anteater proud.

WHO IS HE? ALF is short for Alien Life Form. His real name is Gordon Shumway and he comes from the planet Melmac. He was born on 28 October in the Earth year of 1756, the son of Flo and Bob Shumway. Alf studied sport, art and dentistry at Melmac High School. He also played bouilabaseball (a kind of baseball using fish instead of balls) for three years.

HOW DID HE ARRIVE? His spaceship, similar to a racing car in design, crash-landed on Earth in 1986. It smashed into the suburban home of the Tanner family and they adopted him during his stay on Earth.

LIFESTYLE: Alf seemingly lost his manners somewhere in the upper atmosphere. He blurts out opinions every time he opens his 230-year-old mouth. Alf eats 16 meals a day and his favourite food is domestic cats.

MOST LIKELY TO SAY: "No problem."

CONEHEADS

APPEARANCE: Humanoid, with huge, bald, cone-shaped heads.

PLANET OF ORIGIN: Remulak – part of a binary star system.

WHO ARE THEY? Beldar (male) and Prymaat (female) were sent to Earth in their starcruiser to seize control and put an end to human wars. However, their spacecraft crashed into Lake Michigan, ending their grand plan and trapping them on Earth for many years. Taking the names Fred and Joyce Conehead, they settled in New Jersey where they have raised their daughter Connie.

COVER STORY: They explain away the strange shape of their heads by telling people they are from France.

STRENGTHS: They have three rows of teeth and can eat light bulbs, toilet paper and other household goods. They have a lifespan of between 100–125 Earth years.

ENEMIES: They have been hassled and pursued by Gorman Seeding, a government immigration agent who believes (rightly) that they have entered the country illegally.

* *

D R AND QUINCH

WHO ARE THEY? Waldo D R Dobbs (the 'D R' stands for 'Diminished Responsibility') and Ernest Errol Quinch are alien college students. They are usually to be found surrounded by guns, flame throwers and tactical nuclear weapons. The dangerous twosome's favourite hobby is the complete destruction of their surroundings and everyone else's.

>>>

ALIEN TOURISTS & EXPLORERS

WARNING: They are a danger to any inhabited planet. (Or space station, or ship, etc, etc.)

MOST LIKELY TO SAY: "We're fantastically, incredibly sorry for all of these extremely unreasonable things we did. I can only plead that my simple, barely sentient friend and myself are underprivileged, deprived and also college students. We sincerely want to grow up and change our responsible ways... and I'm not just saying that."

* *

ET

SPECIES: Unknown.

OCCUPATION: Alien explorer. He was accidentally abandoned on Earth by his comrades when humans disturbed them during a plant-collecting expedition.

He was found in a garage on the outskirts of Los Angeles by Elliot, a young boy sensitive to the creature's plight. Elliot took the creature in and taught his extraterrestrial friend to speak English. Escaping the government agents on their trail, Elliot eventually helped reunite ET with his shipmates.

APPEARANCE: Wrinkle-skinned alien with an extendible neck, long arms and large endearing eyes. The creature has a 'heart-light' which glows during moments of strong emotion.

LIFESTYLE: As a race, ETs are rumoured to be keen botanists who study and catalogue the plants and vegetation of many worlds.

STRENGTHS: ET has limited telepathic powers and can also levitate objects and people.

BATTLE TACTICS: Being unbearably cute.

ENEMIES: Government agents led by 'Keys' who want to capture and study ET for their own ends.

MOST LIKELY TO SAY: "ET phone home." "Be good." "Ouch!"

* *

FAIRIES

CATEGORY: UFO report.

DATE: 4 January 1979.

LOCATION: Rowley Regis, England.

WITNESSES: Jean Hingley, factory worker.

APPEARANCE:
The witness reported seeing and speaking with three beings, each about one metre tall. The beings hovered and flew using large fairy-style wings. They had glittering black eyes and wore a goldfish bowl-style breathing-helmet over their heads. They wore silver uniforms with six buttons on each.

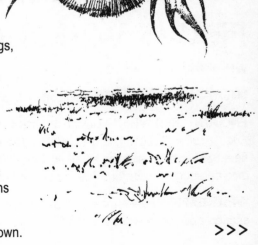

PLANET OF ORIGIN: Unknown.

>>>

ENCOUNTERED WHEN? Having seen her husband off to work, Jean Hingley became aware of an orange sphere about three metres across hovering over her garden. Mrs Hingley's dog was suddenly rendered unconscious as three figures floated past her and into the house.

For the next hour, Mrs Hingley was the unexpected host to three aliens who flew around examining the contents of her home. At one point, the creatures used a laser beam to burn her on the forehead and to blind her temporarily.

WEAKNESSES: The beings seemed afraid of fire and were alarmed by Mrs Hingley lighting a cigarette.

AFTER-EFFECTS: The beings floated back to their ship which took off and headed due north. Mrs Hingley was left exhausted and frightened and suffered from sore eyes for weeks afterwards. The craft left deep track marks in the snow in the garden which extended all the way down into the soil underneath. The case became known as the 'Mince-pie Martians' after the seasonal food that Mrs Hingley offered the aliens to eat.

* *

FERRIS WHEEL

WHAT WAS IT? Alien spacecraft witnessed by Michelle Goddard.

LOCATION: Shepton Mallet, England.

ENCOUNTERED WHEN? Driving through the countryside at twilight on 15 August 1985, Michelle and her partner suddenly spotted what appeared to be a Ferris wheel hovering about 30 metres over a hill. The craft had a metallic structure with red, blue, green, and orange lights around it.

WHAT HAPPENED? After a period of ten seconds, the craft twisted and suddenly disappeared as if it had flown into another dimension.

GALAXY BEING

WHAT WAS IT? Nitrogen-based alien from the Outer Limits of the Andromeda Galaxy. It was accidentally drawn to Earth when a radio-station worker in the USA increased the transmission power being used in a communications experiment.

WHAT HAPPENED? The creature caused several human deaths because of radiation. Rather than return and face trouble at home, it chose disintegration instead. A noble but tragic visitor to Earth.

* *

GIANTS

CATEGORY: UFO report.

DATE: 21 September – 28 October 1989.

LOCATION: Voronezh, Russia.

WITNESSES: Numerous adults and children in a suburban park.

APPEARANCE: The aliens appeared to be three metres tall, wearing silver suits with copper-coloured boots. The beings had very long arms and a wide, flat head. They seemed to be observing their new surroundings through their three eyes – two white eyes and a central red one.

WHAT HAPPENED? Altogether seven sightings and landings were reported in a period of one month. A large, pink sphere was sighted hovering in the sky. The craft was about 15 metres wide and 6 metres high. The tall alien beings were seen to emerge from the craft, sometimes in the company of smaller robots. A pink mist and strange disappearances were also reported.

 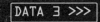

AFTER-EFFECTS: The giants were among the most widely witnessed aliens in Russia. Investigators found that the site "registered very high levels of magnetism" and that the craft had left deep impressions in the ground. From the imprints it was estimated that the object that made them had weighed 11 tonnes.

* *

GOBLINS

CATEGORY: UFO report.

DATE: 21 August 1955.

LOCATION: Kelly-Hopkinsville, Kentucky, USA.

WITNESSES: Eleven members of the Taylor family.

APPEARANCE: Small goblin creatures, about one metre tall. These beings had bald heads with miniature antennae on each side at the top, and large, floppy ears. Their eyes gave out a bright-yellow glow. Their arms and legs were thin. Their fingers ended in sharp, talon-like claws and their feet had suction cups on the bottom.

ENCOUNTERED WHEN? Billy Ray Taylor and Elmer Sutton had seen a UFO earlier in the evening. Around 8 o'clock they opened the kitchen door of their farmhouse to see what their dog was barking at. To their great surprise, they saw a goblin walking towards the house. >>>

Totally ignoring the fact that its arms were raised in a gesture of surrender, the two scared farmers fired a shotgun at the creature. It seemed to absorb the impact, somersaulting backwards into the surrounding bushes.

This was just the beginning. More of the creatures emerged from the darkness and began clambering over the roof of the farmhouse. The encounter lasted right through the night until the first rays of dawn sent the beings scurrying back to their ship.

ALIEN ADVICE: Sadly, they never had the chance to offer any. Certainly, the aliens' report to their home world must have singled out Earth as one of the most unwelcoming planets in the cosmos.

AFTER-EFFECTS: The family endured sleepless nights for several weeks afterwards, as well as the ridicule of the local townspeople for speaking about their amazing story.

As far as we know, there were no other after-effects, although it is quite possible that an enormous alien battle fleet from the creatures' home world is even now en route to Earth for revenge.

* *

GRAAN'S EXPLORERS

CATEGORY: UFO report.

LOCATION: Loxton, South Africa.

WITNESSES: Dannie Van Graan.

APPEARANCE: Small entities of very slim build, with light hair and slanting eyes.

MISSION: Exploration.

>>>

GRAAN'S EXPLORERS

PLANET OF ORIGIN: Unknown.

ENCOUNTERED WHEN? Walking along the flood-protection banking for his village, Dannie Van Graan spotted an odd-looking, round object in the middle of a nearby field. It was some kind of spacecraft.

Inside the vehicle Van Graan could see five beings moving around. One of them spotted him approaching and shot some kind of light beam into his face. The craft then quickly took off and disappeared into the sky.

AFTER-EFFECTS: Van Graan suffered from a nosebleed and blurred vision for a time after the incident.

There were unidentifiable footprints found in the area where the craft had been seen and no plant life grew on the landing site for several years.

* *

HAIRY DWARFS

CATEGORY: UFO report.

DATE: 28 November 1954.

LOCATION: Caracas, Venezuela.

WITNESSES: José Ponce and Gustave Gonzáles.

APPEARANCE: Short creatures covered with dark body hair, with claws for hands.

MISSION: Scientific study of geological samples.

ENCOUNTERED WHEN? The witnesses were driving to a nearby town at 2.00 am when they came across a glowing object about three metres long.

Stopping their car to investigate, they were surprised to see a small, hairy humanoid coming towards them. The witnesses tried to grab the creature, but it escaped. Two more of the tiny figures were seen running back towards the craft carrying rock and soil samples.

AFTER-EFFECTS: The witnesses tried again to capture the first creature, but it used its claws to scratch them. One of the aliens from the craft shot a thin beam of light at them and the first creature made good its escape into the craft, which rose quickly and flew away.

HOWARD THE DUCK

WHO IS HE? Talking duck from another dimension, where Earth is called Duckworld and intelligent fowl are the dominant race. Howard is almost one metre tall, covered in white feathers, has webbed feet and a rather argumentative personality (i.e. he's a pain in the neck). A shift in the cosmic axis caused Howard to fall into our dimension, in the Everglades of Florida. He has been stuck on Earth ever since.

MOST LIKELY TO SAY: "Waaugh!"

TRAPPED IN A WORLD HE NEVER MADE

* *

THE IRON GIANT

WHAT WAS IT? Metal robot 20 metres tall which crash-landed in America. It was suspected of being a weapon from cold war Russia. The Iron Giant ate metal and found that junkyard cars were particularly tasty. He was befriended by human Hogarth Hughes who helped him escape capture by the authorities. It was revealed that the Iron Giant was the product of an advanced civilisation from the stars.

KLAATU AND GORT

SPECIES: Klaatu – humanoid alien diplomat. Gort – tall, silver robot.

PLANET OF ORIGIN: Said to be 250 million miles from Earth, although this may well be an underestimate, designed to keep the true location secret.

MISSION: Klaatu's huge, silver saucer landed in Washington DC causing great alarm in military and media circles.

Eventually, Klaatu emerged from the ship with his loyal robot Gort, but was shot by a trigger-happy soldier. The wounded alien was rushed to hospital, but recovered quickly and made his escape.

Posing as 'Mr Carpenter', Klaatu took a room at a boarding house where he met Helen Benson and her son Bobby. Thanks to his close contact with the people around him, Klaatu soon began to discover more about the human condition.

WHAT HAPPENED? He secretly met with top scientists to arrange a practical demonstration of his people's technology and power. In an incident that became known as The Day the Earth Stood Still, Klaatu arranged for all non-essential electrical power to stop working everywhere on the planet.

Klaatu's presence was betrayed by Helen's jealous boyfriend and he was shot and killed by the panicking authorities.

Helen had to make the most important journey in human history as she rushed to Washington to pass on Klaatu's dying words to Gort – the only words that would stop him destroying the planet.

Having received the the message – "*Klaatu barada nikto*" – Gort sadly retrieved his master's body watched by shame-faced humans. The pair left with a warning that human violence must stop if the Earth is to survive.

KLAATU AND GORT

LAVENDER FIELD ALIENS

CATEGORY: UFO report.

DATE: 1 July 1965.

LOCATION: Valensole, France.

WITNESSES: Farmer Maurice Masse.

APPEARANCE: A variation of the Greys (see page 21) – about one metre tall, with a large head, big, dark eyes and a lipless mouth. They wore one-piece green suits and spoke to each other with gutteral sounds.

ENCOUNTERED WHEN? Alerted by a high-pitched noise at 6.00 one morning, Masse spotted a strange object in the middle of his lavender field. It was a landing craft shaped like an egg about 5 metres wide. The craft had six legs and stood in the field rather like a giant spider.

Masse saw what he took to be two young boys near the craft, gathering lavender, and approached them. As he got closer, he realised that the figures were not human. One of the beings pointed a rod at Masse and he suddenly found himself completely paralysed.

They climbed back inside their craft and took off. Masse remained paralysed for 20 minutes after they left.

MISSION: Peaceful, scientific research. Masse felt no fear of the creatures and thought that they were just as curious about him as he was about them.

AFTER-EFFECTS: Masse found that he needed much more sleep than usual for the next few weeks – a common symptom after a close encounter. But Masse got off lightly in comparison to the landing site, which remained completely barren of lavender plants for the next decade.

MINIATURE EXPLORERS

CATEGORY: UFO report.

DATE: 19 August 1970.

LOCATION: Penang, Malaysia.

WITNESSES: David Tan, Mohamed Zulkifli and four other schoolboys aged between 8 and 11 years.

APPEARANCE: Aliens eight centimetres tall landed in a flying saucer the size of a dinner plate.

MISSION: Exploration.

ENCOUNTERED WHEN? The group of boys were playing near their school when they spotted the miniature craft landing. They watched as five tiny aliens emerged and began to look around – seemingly their first time on the planet. The aliens' faces resembled ugly animals and they carried tiny weapons.

One of the boys attempted to capture the alien leader and pick him up. The tiny creature's response was to fire his weapon and the other boys ran away to get help. Returning to the scene with a schoolteacher, they found their unconscious friend but no sign of the ship or its tiny crew.

AFTER-EFFECTS: The alien weapon had left a red mark on the boy's leg, but otherwise he was unharmed. Despite suggestions that the boys had watched one too many episodes of *Land of the Giants*, they all insisted their story was true.

The boys' report was one of a wave of similar sightings of miniature aliens in Malaysia that summer. The truth is out there, it seems. It's just very, very small.

MINIATURE EXPLORERS

MONOLITH

WHAT IS IT? Mysterious, black, rectangular slab that appeared on Earth four million years ago and assisted the evolution of apes into humans. Another monolith was uncovered on the moon in the late 20th century.

PLANET OF ORIGIN: Still unknown.

WHAT HAPPENED? It sent a message towards Jupiter. A space mission to Jupiter to learn the target of the message went wrong when the ship's computer HAL malfunctioned and it tried to kill the crew.

MORK

WHO IS HE? Humanoid from the planet Ork.

Mork's spacecraft resembles a white egg and first landed outside the city of Boulder, Colorado, USA, where he met the human Mindy McConnell. At the time of his arrival, Mork was wearing a red jumpsuit with a triangle on its chest.

LIFESTYLE: Mork sits on his head and drinks through his fingers.

MISSION: Mork was sent to Earth to study humans. He reports back to his planet's leader, Orsen, often addressing him in such terms as "Your Imperial Vastness".

WHAT HAPPENED? Mork became a lodger in Mindy's home. They eventually fell in love and got married. Mork gave birth to a middle-aged son called Mearth.

MOST LIKELY TO SAY: "Na-nu, na-nu." "Shazbot."

* *

MR MXYZPTLK

APPEARANCE: Short, elf-like figure.

WHO IS HE? Mr Mxyzptlk (pronounced mix-yez-pittle-ick) is an entity from the fifth dimension who considers it his duty to annoy Superman as much as he possibly can – which is really quite a lot.

POWERS: Mr Mxyzptlk's superpowers are actually based on science but are so advanced that they seem more like magic. Superman usually defeats him by sharp thinking, rather than brute strength.

THE NIAGARA ALIENS

CATEGORY: UFO report.

DATE: January 1958.

LOCATION: New York State Thruway, near Niagara Falls, USA.

WITNESSES: Wished to remain anonymous.

APPEARANCE: "They seemed to be like animals with four legs and a tail, but with two front feelers under the head, like arms."

ENCOUNTERED WHEN? Driving through a snowstorm very late one night to see her son, the witness came across what she thought was an aircraft wreck in the middle of the otherwise deserted highway.

At first, she could not work out what it was she was looking at, but as she got nearer, her headlights died, the engine stalled and the car drifted to a halt. She looked up into the swirling snow and saw two aliens suspended in the air over the craft, apparently repairing an illuminated rod-like device about 20 metres long. The entities then vanished as the saucer-shaped ship rose off the road surface and disappeared into the heavy snowstorm above.

MISSION: Repairing their own ship, possibly from damage caused by the bad weather.

AFTER-EFFECTS: As soon as the craft was gone, the witness's car started again and she was able to continue on her journey. She also reported a hole melted in the snow where the craft had landed. This area was still warm to the touch minutes after the ship's departure.

NIAGARA ALIENS

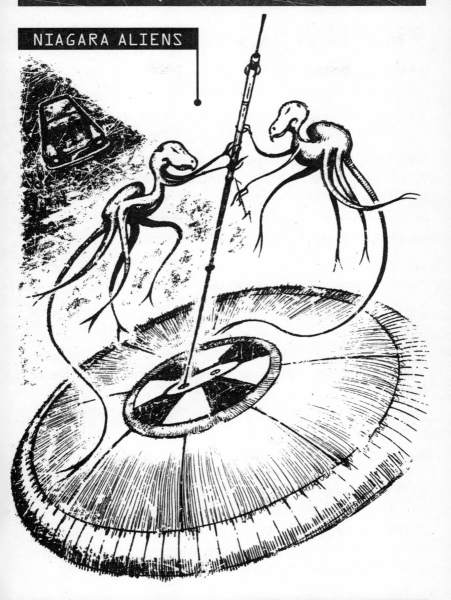

PREDATORS

APPEARANCE: Humanoid aliens over two metres tall, with large tusks on their faces and dreadlock-style, black spikes.

WHO ARE THEY? Predators travel the galaxy in search of worthy opponents to hunt (i.e. they have far too much time on their hands).

WEAPONS: Predators wear special camouflage armour that changes like a chameleon to match its background, making the aliens almost invisible to their enemies. Normally, they carry a spear-like weapon. A Predator's other combat equipment includes miniature nuclear bombs.

STRENGTHS: Fast-moving and stronger than humans.

WEAKNESSES: Predators do not see particularly well in normal Earth daylight, preferring to hunt their prey using infra-red, heat vision.

BATTLE TACTICS: Predators have visited many planets to enjoy the thrill of the hunt. At least two Predator expeditions to Earth have been recorded – both ending in the death of the alien hunter.

Major Alan 'Dutch' Schaefer fought one of the creatures in the jungles of Central America. Although the alien claimed the lives of most of Dutch's men, the Major defeated the creature in combat after finding that a covering of mud could be used to confuse the alien's infra-red vision.

Another Predator was killed by Los Angeles policeman Michael Harrigan after it had murdered a number of criminals. Other Predators appeared at the death of their comrade; they decided that Harrigan had beaten him fairly and departed peacefully.

CLASSIFIED DATA: It is believed that the Predator involved in the LA incident had the head of an 'alien' displayed in its trophy room, indicating a past conflict between those two famous species.

RIGELIANS

APPEARANCE: Green, tentacled aliens, often seen drooling excessively.

WHO ARE THEY? Kang and Kodos are visitors to Earth from Rigel IV. They encountered the Simpson family in the middle of a family barbecue and offered to take Homer, Marge and the kids to their home planet – "a world of infinite delights to tantalise your senses and challenge your intellectual limitations".

LIFESTYLE: Their flying saucer's entertainment centre receives over one million television channels from the furthest reaches of the galaxy.

LANGUAGE: Rigelian – which "by an astonishing coincidence" is exactly the same as English.

GREAT MISTAKES: During the voyage to Rigel IV, Lisa began to suspect that the aliens were planning to cook and eat them all upon their arrival. Sneaking around the ship, she discovered a book called *How to Cook Humans* and ran to warn her family. Embarrassingly, the full title of the book was revealed as *How to Cook for Forty Humans* and the Simpsons were dumped back on Earth.

The deeply offended Rigelians explained: "We offered you paradise. You would have experienced emotions a hundred times greater than what you call love. And a thousand times greater than what you call fun. You would have been treated like gods and lived forever in beauty. But, now, because of your distrustful nature, that can never be."

As Marge observed: "For a superior race, they really like to rub it in."

* *

ROBOTS

CATEGORY: UFO report.

DATE: 10 September 1954. This sighting was part of a wave all over the country that year.

LOCATION: Quarouble, France.

WITNESSES: Marius Dewilde.

APPEARANCE: Short, robotic entities wearing diving bell-type suits without any visible arms.

PLANET OF ORIGIN: Unknown.

ENCOUNTERED WHEN? Alerted by the barking of his dog late one evening, Dewilde left his house to check the garden for intruders.

Switching on the outside lights, he was shocked to find two strange humanoids wandering in his garden. In the distance he could see some kind of craft that had landed on nearby railway tracks.

Dewilde attempted to grab one of the little beings, but he was paralysed by a very bright light from their spacecraft.

ALIEN ADVICE: None given, but after the attempted assault, would probably advise other aliens to avoid landing in France.

MISSION: Peaceful exploration.

AFTER-EFFECTS: By the time Dewilde found he could move again, the craft had taken off and disappeared.

A few days later investigators arrived to look into the sighting and discovered damage to the railway line that could only have been caused by an object weighing 30 tonnes.

* *

ROSWELL ALIENS

WHO ARE THEY? Max Evens, his sister Isabel and his best friend Michael Guerin pretend to be human but are really aliens abandoned on Earth after their ship crashed in 1947 in the dusty town of Roswell, New Mexico. A fourth alien, Tess Harding, later joined the group, with whom Max felt an inexplicable connection.

WHAT HAPPENED? Max risked exposing his alien identity when he used his healing powers to save the life of Liz Parker following a gunshot wound. The aliens later discover that they are in fact some sort of alien-human hybrid reincarnated from genetic material. In their past existence, Max was a king and Isabel was indeed his sister; Michael was his second in command and Tess was his wife.

SPEC-TRUMS

WHO ARE THEY? Race of friendly aliens who can travel through space without the need of a ship by forming themselves into a sphere of energy.

WHAT HAPPENED? They visited Earth and found that our atmosphere gave them the power to change the colours of any object they touched. The first human the Spec-trums encountered was Kevin, now better known throughout most of the universe as Cosmic Kev.

* *

MATTHEW STAR

WHO IS HE? Son of the deposed King of the planet Quadris, who came to Earth to escape his father's enemies. Star has telepathic powers and becomes an undercover agent for the Air Force in return for his continued freedom.

* *

STONE-HEADED ALIEN

CATEGORY: UFO report.

DATE: Autumn 1972 – Summer 1973.

LOCATION: Argentina, South America.

APPEARANCE: Tall humanoid with facial features and head-shape similar to the statues on Easter Island (i.e. with a very long face and chin).

WITNESSES: The being was seen by many witnesses during a seven-month UFO flap in Argentina.

ENCOUNTERED WHEN? Eduardo Fernando Dedeu was driving home very late at night when his radio began malfunctioning. Stopping to fix it, he noticed a hitchhiker standing on the opposite side of the road and offered him a lift.

A short time later, the car lost all power and came to a sudden halt as Dedeu saw a white and green UFO hovering over a nearby field.

Dedeu stared at the object and by the time he looked around, his hitchhiker had left the car and vanished – leaving a broken door handle behind as he made his escape.

MISSION: There are two obvious possibilities:

1/ The alien was hitchhiking back to a rendezvous with his ship.

2/ The alien was trying to escape from his shipmates, hoping to hitchhike away from the ship, and escaping when it was sighted again.

ALIEN ADVICE: None given; the being answered Dedeu's questions with meaningless grunts and sounds.

* *

THIRD ROCK FROM THE SUN ALIENS

APPEARANCE: While on Earth they are disguised as humans.

WHO ARE THEY? Team of four explorers sent to Earth to observe and learn about human life. Taking human form, the four aliens took up residence in Rutherford, Ohio and became the Solomon family.

Dick Solomon is their leader and High Commander. He teaches physics at a local university. Known for being hopelessly gullible when dealing with Earthlings. Since his arrival, Dick has fallen in love with human Mary Albright and they have enjoyed an on-off-on-off-on-off relationship ever since.

Sally Solomon is Dick's second in command. She is a tough, male lieutenant who sees women as the inferior sex and resents having to use a female identity.

Harry Solomon is the really weird one. He can act as a transmitter when Dick talks to Giant Big Head, their leader.

Tommy Solomon is actually the oldest of the four aliens, but has been forced to use the body of a teenage boy for his stay on Earth.

KNOWN HUMAN ASSOCIATES:

Dr Mary Albright also works at the university. She shares her office (and sometimes more) with Dick.

Mrs Dubcek is the unfortunate landlady from whom the aliens rent their attic accommodation.

Officer Don is one of Rutherford's policemen and has a not-so-secret passion for the gorgeous Sally.

LIFESTYLE: The aliens are constantly struggling to understand and fit into human society. Their new human bodies are continuing sources of fascination – for them, a simple sneeze is a major event.

WEAKNESSES: Almost everything.

* *

THE WATCHER

NAME: Uatu.

SPECIES: Unknown – but his home world is in another galaxy.

OCCUPATION: The ultimate tourist, the Watcher is an ageless observer of events in Earth's solar system.

APPEARANCE: Tall, bald-headed humanoid.

LIFESTYLE: The Watcher lives alone in the 'Blue Area' on the far side of Earth's moon. His time is spent recording all important events that take place in the Sol system.

Watchers are telepathic and can scan the minds of nearly all known life forms. The entire Watcher race now lives scattered across the cosmos observing the unfolding histories of the younger races.

>>>

Like Time Lords, the Watchers have a strict code of not interfering in the affairs of others. Like Time Lords, they break it frequently.

EARTH ALLIES: The Fantastic Four, the Avengers.

MOST LIKELY TO SAY: "Emulate the Watcher! Stand and observe!"

* *

ZAPHOD BEEBLEBROX

Title: President of the Imperial Galactic Government.

APPEARANCE: Two-headed humanoid.

OCCUPATION: Adventurer, self-publicist, ex-hippy.

AGE: 200 – or so he claims.

PLANET OF ORIGIN: Betelgeuse V.

KNOWN ASSOCIATES: Ford Prefect, Arthur Dent, Trillion.

CLAIM TO FAME: Stealing the *Heart of Gold* spacecraft with its brand new Improbability Drive and (as listed in *The Hitch Hiker's Guide to the Galaxy*) being voted Worst Dressed Sentient Being in the Known Universe an incredible seven times.

MOST LIKELY TO SAY: "That is really amazing. That really is truly amazing. That is so amazingly amazing I think I'd like to steal it."

DATA 3 COMPLETE

ALIEN SHAPESHIFTERS

DATA 1
DATA 2
DATA 3
DATA 4
DATA 5
DATA 6
DATA 7
DATA 8
DATA 9
DATA 10

Shapeshifters generally have something of a shady reputation within the galactic community. With species like the Skrulls and the Founders included in their number, perhaps that's not surprising.

Most inhabited worlds have dark folk tales about evil doppelgangers, or doubles, replacing friends or loved ones. Such stories almost certainly have their roots in early and unorganised planetary exploration by the Skrull Empire.

Much of the modern fear of shapeshifters is unfair and unfounded, but the wise, interstellar traveller should be familiar with the following species and individuals:

>>>

THE COLOR OUT OF SPACE

WHAT IS IT? Shapeless entity that fell to Earth inside a meteorite in June 1882. It was first seen as a coloured globule, then later as a cloud of vapour, before changing again into slimy ooze.

PLANET OF ORIGIN: Unknown.

HISTORY: The creature known only as the Color out of Space crash-landed on farmland in Arkham, Massachusetts, USA. Investigators sent to examine the fallen meteorite discovered several coloured globules deep inside its stony bulk. One of these released the deadly Color which began to feed on the colours in its surroundings, draining them to a dull grey. It affected places, things, vegetation and, worst of all, people. The flesh of its victims slowly turned into a grey, brittle material, which disintegrated into dust while they were still alive.

WHAT HAPPENED? Having drained the colour and life out of everyone on the farm, the entity returned to space amid a colourful and bizarre light show which lit up the countryside for several miles around. Its actions were recorded by historian of the strange, H P Lovecraft.

* *

DIRE WRAITHS

APPEARANCE: Shapechangers. Their usual ploy is to try and invade a world quietly, gradually replacing people in positions of power with their own agents in the form of exact duplicates.

WHO ARE THEY? The Dire Wraiths are a branch of the Skrull race (see page 93). They were driven out of Skrull space because of their practice of "dire, dark magicks" – i.e. alien black magic. The Dire Wraiths can

shapeshift in the same way as Skrulls. They also have the ability to absorb the personal memories of other life forms by sucking out their brains. Dire Wraiths possess a powerful combination of alien science and black magic.

HISTORY: Having left Skrull space, the Dire Wraiths made a chaotic region of space called the Dark Nebula their new home, where they set about attempting to invade their nearby neighbours. When the Dire Wraiths launched their attack, the planet Galador fought back by creating cyborg Spaceknights under the leadership of Rom (see page 118). The heroic Spaceknights scattered the Wraiths throughout the universe. Unable to return to the Dark Nebula, the Wraiths set out to secretly infiltrate other more backward worlds, including the planet Earth.

LIFESTYLE: In the 200 years they roamed the universe, the Dire Wraiths committed numerous atrocities, bringing death and destruction to untold millions. (They also owe money in several, well-known galactic restaurants.)

MOST LIKELY TO SAY: "Your sentimental emotionalism has doomed you! We Wraiths know nothing of love – that is why our hatred shall triumph in the end!" (Yep, they really do speak like that.)

WHAT HAPPENED? They were finally defeated by the combined efforts of Earth superheroes like the Avengers and the X-Men, but travellers are warned that the odd Wraith outpost may still exist in the backwaters of the galaxy.

* *

FOUNDERS

WHO ARE THEY? The Founders of the evil Dominion (their equivalent of the Federation) are shapeshifters, also called changelings. They rule the Gamma Quadrant and have invasion plans that include

Federation space, thanks to their use of the wormhole near Deep Space Nine. The Dominion has existed for over 2000 years.

They are a silicate-based life form, capable of metamorphosing cell structure. They can change their physical shape to resemble any person or any item. However, they must return to a liquid state to regenerate at regular intervals.

MOST FAMOUS FACE: Deep Space Nine's security chief Odo was found floating near an asteroid belt, many years ago, with no memory of where he had come from. He was later revealed to be a Founder/changeling.

MOST LIKELY TO SAY: "It's too late. We're everywhere."

WARNING: The Federation is currently at war with the Dominion and any tourists who choose to travel to the Gamma Quadrant do so entirely at their own risk.

* *

HELLHOUNDS

WHAT ARE THEY: Used by the Dire Wraiths to hunt their enemies. Hellhounds are normal Earth dogs that have been mutated into hideous, shapeshifting beasts by the Wraiths' black magic.

* *

IMPOSSIBLE MAN

WHO IS HE? Native of the planet Poppup who used his bizarre, shapechanging powers to annoy the Fantastic Four. Later he made the Impossible Woman out of a part of his own body and the two left together to set up their own world.

MARTIANS

WHO ARE THEY? Humanoids with dark skins and golden eyes. They are slender in build and used to breathing in an atmosphere with little oxygen. They sometimes travel in canopies pulled through the red skies of Mars by flamebirds. Their dwellings are often made from crystal architecture (like those of the Minbari – a race similar in many ways).

POWERS: As detailed in the *Martian Chronicles*, the race is highly telepathic. Martians are open to the thoughts of all those around them. This has been known to lead to mental problems and even insanity.

Although not true shapeshifters, they can project telepathic illusions difficult to tell from the real thing. They have appeared to unsuspecting settlers as lost or dead relatives.

CANALS: In past ages, the Martians had a planet-wide network of canals on which they sailed their beautiful ships.

EARTH EXPEDITIONS: The Martians are now a dying race, their beautiful, crystal cities long since fallen into ruin, but even so the survivors have been known to resist outsiders. The first three expeditions from Earth all met with failure. The first rocket's crew fell victim to a jealous Martian husband, and the second and third expeditions also met with violent ends.

Tragically for the Martians, however, the third expedition brought chicken-pox to Mars; this spread through the population like wildfire, killing almost the entire race. After this, the fourth expedition from Earth had some limited success and established the beginnings of a settlement on Mars.

MOST LIKELY TO BE DESCRIBED AS: "They had a house of crystal pillars on the planet Mars by the edge of an empty sea, and every morning you could see Mrs K eating the golden fruits that grew from the crystal walls..."

NOTE: Native Martians are now so rare that visitors are asked to report any sightings to the Ylla Research Centre, Iron Town, Mars.

* *

MARTIAN MANHUNTER

WHO IS HE? Green-skinned Martian with the ability to change his shape, fly, become invisible and read minds, among many other things. He is a member of the influential Justice League of America along with Superman and Batman. His main weakness is fire in any form.

MAYA

SPECIES: Psychon.

APPEARANCE: A babe.

WHO IS SHE? The daughter of Mentor from the planet Psychon. Mentor attempted to trap Moonbase Alpha's Commander Koenig and feed him into his biological computer Psyche. When her home world was destroyed, Maya elected to join Moonbase Alpha becoming its resident science officer.

STRENGTHS: Maya is a shapeshifter, or metamorph, who can become any animal at will – although she can only remain in that form for a maximum of one hour.

ENEMIES: The Dorcons. They hunt Psychons for their brain stems, which they use to become immortal.

* *

SALT MONSTER
(AKA M-133 CREATURE OR SALT VAMPIRE)

WHAT WAS IT? Solitary survivor from a now extinct race. This life form needed salt to survive which it extracted from its human victims. It was also able to change shape and take on the form of any of its victims. This enabled it to hide in plain sight as it waited for the chance to feed again.

WHAT HAPPENED? The last known example of the species was killed when it invaded Captain Kirk's *Enterprise*.

SKRULLS

APPEARANCE: Green-skinned, humanoid reptiles with large, pointed ears.

WHO ARE THEY? Shapechanging aliens with a huge space empire consisting of much of the Andromeda Galaxy. The Skrulls evolved over ten million years ago.

>>>

PLANET OF ORIGIN: A semitropical world called Skrullos in the Drox system of Andromeda. Later, the Skrulls moved their 'throneworld' to the planet Tarnax IV. This world was recently destroyed by Galactus, an event which plunged their empire into utter chaos.

STRENGTHS: Shapechanging abilities, advanced starships and weapons.

WEAKNESSES: Their eyesight is inferior to that of humans and they are not good at improvising battle plans or thinking on their feet.

BATTLE TACTICS: The Skrulls were originally traders interested mostly in business, but attacks from the growing Kree Empire forced them to become more military-minded.

ALIEN ARTEFACT: The Cosmic Cube – a reality-altering invention of the Skrull Empire. Eventually became an intelligent life form in its own right and rebelled against them, destroying many of their worlds.

ENEMIES: Involved in war with the Kree for millions of years. Have repeatedly shown an interest in invading the Earth, but have been halted by Earth heroes – the Fantastic Four and the Avengers.

WARNING: Travellers are advised that the Skulls are considered an unreliable and untrustworthy race. Any citizens of Earth who enter into trade or other agreements with them do so entirely at their own risk.

* *

THE THING

WHAT IS IT? Deadly alien that can form itself into a duplicate of any person or animal by contaminating them with its own blood. It is able to infiltrate any camp or dwelling of its prey and is almost impossible to kill,

making the Thing a very dangerous enemy.

SECURITY MEASURES: One way of detecting a disguised Thing is to take a blood sample and subject it to an electric shock. If the blood belongs to a Thing, it will recoil from the electricity.

HOW DID IT GET TO EARTH? The original Thing became trapped on Earth in a past age when the propulsion drives on its spacecraft malfunctioned because of the Earth's magnetic field. Its craft crash-landed in the Antarctic, where it froze and lay trapped in ice until revived by members of a modern-day Polar expedition. The Thing was eventually killed; however, humanity can only hope that others of its species do not come looking for their lost comrade.

WARNING: The Thing is one of the most dangerous life forms in the entire galaxy. To knowingly import any member of the species on to an inhabited planet carries a death sentence in most star systems.

* *

VAMPIRELLA

WHO IS SHE? Vampire-like female who can change into a bat. It is believed she travelled to Earth from the planet Draculon, where the inhabitants drank and washed in free-flowing blood instead of water.

Vampirella survives on Earth by drinking a synthetic blood serum.

FASHION SENSE: Usually wears a skimpy, red bikini and little else.

ZYGONS

WHO WERE THEY? Shapechanging aliens who landed their crippled spacecraft in Loch Ness, Scotland.

PLANET OF ORIGIN: Their home world was destroyed in a stellar explosion after they left.

MISSION: Using the monstrous Skarasen and their own ability to take on the features of any human they chose, they planned to take over the Earth. Sadly for them, their attempt at world domination brought them into conflict with the forces of UNIT and its mysterious scientific adviser, the Doctor.

STRENGTHS: Their technology used 'organic crystallography'.

BATTLE TACTICS: Their leader Broton took on a human disguise to infiltrate the World Energy Conference in an attempt to destroy it. He was shot by UNIT troops and killed.

ALLIES: The Skarasen – a huge, aquatic, cyborg beast created by the Zygons that lived in Loch Ness. It was sometimes spotted by curious locals and gave rise to the legend of the Loch Ness Monster.

DATA 4 COMPLETE

ALIEN ALLIES

DATA 1
DATA 2
DATA 3
DATA 4
DATA 5
DATA 6
DATA 7
DATA 8
DATA 9
DATA 10

Once a space traveller has watched their home world shrink to a pinpoint of faint light and then blink out altogether in the empty darkness of the vast universe, he or she may begin to feel rather lost and alone (maybe even teary-eyed). On such occasions, it is good to know who your friends are. For example, would a Draconian ambassador or a cuddly Ewok make a better travelling companion on a long, economy space flight?

Data File 5 lists the races and creatures that Earth can think of as its allies out there in the great beyond. It also offers helpful hints on how not to offend members of the Minbari race and why you should never take a Mon Calamari to a fish restaurant.

>>>

ASHTAR

CATEGORY: UFO/contactee report.

DATE: 18 July 1952.

LOCATION: Giant Rock, California, USA.

WITNESSES: George Van Tassel was born in Ohio in 1910. Always fascinated by flight, Van Tassel worked on and around aircraft for much of his life.

APPEARANCE: Human except for having a 'higher vibratory level' than mere Earthlings.

PLANET OF ORIGIN: Alpha Centauri.

ENCOUNTERED WHEN? When he moved to Giant Rock, Van Tassel began receiving telepathic messages about the Inter-Galactic Federation and the United Council of the Universal Brotherhood. He claimed that the messages were from an entity in space.

MISSION: To help humanity develop and evolve.

ALIEN ADVICE: "Be good to the planet, be good to each other and don't mess with atomic bombs."

AFTER-EFFECTS: An annual Spacecraft Convention was held for many years afterwards at Giant Rock, attracting crowds of up to 18,000 people.

* *

AURONS

WHO ARE THEY? Humanoid telepaths from the planet Auron. One of their number, Cally, travelled with Blake on board the *Liberator* during his attempts to overthrow Servalan's Terran Federation.

BAJORANS

WHO ARE THEY? Religious race with a distinctive ridge of bone on the bridge of the nose. Their home world Bajor suffered decades of Cardassian occupation, a period that has left its people with many scars. The political leader of Bajor is the First Minister, elected every six years.

MOST FAMOUS FACE: Major Kira Neryls, ex-freedom fighter; now part of the command staff of Deep Space Nine.

ALIEN ARTEFACT: Orbs of the Prophets. These Bajoran religious objects, believed to have been handed down from the Prophets (actually the "wormhole aliens", see page 197). The 12 mystic orbs resemble hourglasses in shape and have different powers; for example, the Orb of Time allows temporal displacement (time travel) to occur.

* *

CHIANA

WHO IS SHE? Young thief who rebelled against the mind-controlled society of her fellow Nebari and left her home planet.

* *

CHOCKY

WHAT WAS SHE? Alien intelligence who wanted to secretly help humankind. Chocky made mental contact with Matthew, a 12-year-old boy, speaking to him as a voice in his head.

PLANET OF ORIGIN: Chocky was from an ancient race who had learned to travel across the vastness of space using their minds instead of physical transportation.

>>>

For a long time Chocky's people believed that they were the only life in the whole universe: "A single, freakish pinpoint of reason in a vast cosmos – utterly lonely in the horrid wastes of space." Whenever Chocky's people discover other life forms, they consider it their sacred duty to nurture them.

MISSION: Chocky's purpose was to influence and stimulate Matthew so that he could discover 'cosmic power' – a source of limitless energy – and thus help humankind.

WHAT HAPPENED? Things went wrong for Chocky when she told Matthew too much too soon and drew the attention of scientists and government agencies. Chocky left Matthew but vowed to carry out her mission with someone else, only next time more carefully.

* *

CLANGERS

APPEARANCE: Pink creatures with large ears who speak in distinctive whistles.

PLANET OF ORIGIN: A small, blue planet similar in appearance to the moon, where they live underground. The entrances to their homes are protected by metal lids. It is the sound of these being slammed shut that gives the Clangers their name.

WHO ARE THEY?

Major Clanger, head of the family, the largest and oldest of the Clangers.
Mother Clanger, who looks after the younger Clangers.
Small Clanger, an explorer, noted for his experiments.
Tiny Clanger, probably the friendliest Clanger.
Granny Clanger, who likes a quiet life knitting with tinsel string.

KNOWN FRIENDS:

The Soup Dragon lives inside the planet near the soup wells and feeds
the Clangers. It has been estimated that there is enough soup in the
soup wells to last the Clangers for 7,384,497,003 years if they
are careful.

>>>

The Froglets are small, orange creatures who live in a lake of pink soup at the centre of the planet. They can make things appear and disappear at will, performing all manner of tricks.

The Iron Chicken lives in a nest made of bits of scrap-metal which she finds during her many travels. She once made Tiny Clanger a radio-hat so that they could communicate at any time.

WEAKNESSES: A fondness for Blue String Pudding.

TRANSPORT: Major Clanger's fishing-boat. This is powered by notes from the Music Trees grown by Tiny Clanger from the last two semiquavers that the Soup Dragon forgot to eat.

MOST LIKELY TO BE INTRODUCED AS: "A long way away, in a far corner of the sky, you can see, on a clear night, a faint, blue-coloured star. It is really a planet but it is such a small and unimportant one that it doesn't have a name. For one family, however, it is a very important place. It is home."

* *

CLOSE ENCOUNTER ALIENS
(AKA THE DEVIL'S TOWER ALIENS)

WHO ARE THEY? Slender, white-skinned, space travellers who landed on Devil's Tower in Wyoming to have their first close encounter of the third kind with humanity.

WHAT HAPPENED? In 1977, the visiting aliens released airmen who were spacenapped in 1944, but had not aged at all since.

The aliens used the shared language of music as a basis for communication and left with several human volunteers on board their huge mothership.

* *

CONE HAT

CATEGORY: UFO report.

DATE: 7 January 1970.

LOCATION: Mikkeli, southern Finland.

WITNESSES: Aaron Heinonen and Esko Viljo.

APPEARANCE: Short humanoid wearing a cone-shaped hat. The metre-tall being had thin arms and legs, with a pale face and a large hook nose.

MISSION: Exploration and perhaps deliberate contact.

ENCOUNTERED WHEN? The witnesses had been out skiing when they saw a round, metallic object descending from the sky. The craft hovered three metres above the ground and a light beam shone down. A figure materialised in the light. The being was holding a small, black box which emitted a yellow light. The figure pointed the box at the humans and a thick, red mist was sprayed out of it, enveloping the pair.

AFTER-EFFECTS: When the mist cleared, the craft and creature were gone and Heinonen began to feel ill. He had head pains, trouble breathing and violent vomiting. Even with proper medical help, he continued to suffer for months with all the symptoms of radiation sickness. Viljo was also ill, although not as badly.

Heinonen claimed he had 23 more UFO encounters with the same species of alien over the next two years.

CONE HAT

DEWBACKS

WHAT ARE THEY? Large, unintelligent, four-legged reptiles ridden by (among others) Imperial Stormtroopers in the sandy wastes of Tatooine.

* *

DRACONIANS

APPEARANCE: Green-skinned humanoids.

WHO ARE THEY? Intelligent and dignified reptiles with a large space empire and many trading routes.

Their society is dynastic and strictly divided into nobles and the ordinary Draconians. Social life is dominated by males; females are not even allowed to speak in the presence of the Emperor.

PLANET OF ORIGIN: Draconia.

STRENGTHS: Intelligence.

WEAKNESSES: Pride – their noblemen will travel only on huge battle cruisers.

POLITICAL TACTICS: In attempting to negotiate a peace accord with the human race, the Emperor sent his son to act as their ambassador.

WEAPONS: Galaxy-class battle cruisers armed with neutronic missiles.

ENEMIES: The Draconian Empire was nearly tricked into going to war with humankind by an unholy alliance between the Daleks and the evil Time Lord, the Master. Only the intervention of the third Doctor and his assistant, Jo Grant, put an end to the scheme.

MOST LIKELY TO SAY: "My life at your command."

DRACONIANS

EWOKS

APPEARANCE: Cute teddy bears about one metre tall.

WHO ARE THEY? The Ewoks befriended Princess Leia and the rebels, and turned the tide of war in their favour during the Battle of Endor.

PLANET OF ORIGIN: Endor's forest moon. The Ewoks live in villages with their dwellings built high above the ground in the trees.

LIFESTYLE: Ewoks hunt food and gather fruit during the day, leaving the dangerous forest at night to retire to the safety of their villages. They love telling tall tales and singing around their campfires. Ewok religion is centred on their giant trees of the forest. They believe the trees to be guardian spirits.

STRENGTHS: Good teamwork and keen understanding of their environment.

WEAPONS: Bow and arrows, spears and simple forest traps.

* *

GREEN LANTERN CORPS

WHO ARE THEY? Created by the Guardians of the Universe, the Green Lantern Corps consists of 3600 individual Green Lanterns sworn to fight evil. Each Green Lantern patrols a particular sector of space.

APPEARANCE: All Green Lanterns have a power ring and a green and black uniform. The Corps consists of an amazing variety of alien life forms. The first Earth Green Lantern was test pilot Hal Jorden.

PLANET OF ORIGIN: Lanterns are chosen from worlds all over the galaxy, making the Corps one of the few truly multispecies organisations anywhere. >>>

STRENGTHS: Their power ring can create any object the owner wills it to.

WEAKNESSES: Each ring must be recharged every 24 hours and has no effect on anything that is yellow in colour.

ENEMIES: The Anti-Monitor.

MOST LIKELY TO SAY: Their oath:

> "In brightest day, in blackest night,
> No evil shall escape my sight.
> Let those who worship evil's might
> Beware my power – Green Lantern's light!"

* *

GUARDIAN OF FOREVER

APPEARANCE: A large, doughnut-shaped portal.

WHAT IS IT? An intelligent time portal, created in the very distant past by an unknown civilisation.

WHAT HAPPENED? An unauthorised trip through the Guardian of Forever by Dr McCoy accidentally resulted in the creation of a future universe where Nazi Germany won World War II, and the starship *Enterprise* and the Federation no longer existed.

Captain Kirk and Mr Spock also had to journey back in time to restore the timeline, which they discovered hinged on the death of one particular women.

ADDITIONAL DATA: The Guardian was used by Mr Spock again during the 'Yesteryear Incident'. He travelled back to his childhood home in the city of Shikahr on Vulcan to prevent his own death at the age of 7.

GUARDIANS OF THE GALAXY

WHO WERE THEY? Team of heroes who defended the Earth against the invading Badoons in the 31st century. Members included Vance Astro, Charlie 27, Marinex and Yondu.

* *

GUNGANS

WHO ARE THEY? Humaniod amphibious species with powerful lungs, capable of holding their breath for long periods. Gungans are as comfortable in water as they are on dry land. There are a number of Gungan races, but most tend to be tall and lanky with very expressive and flexible faces.

PLANET OF ORIGIN: Naboo.

FAMOUS FACE: The best known Gungan in the universe is the incredibly annoying Jar Jar Binks. Jar Jar speak maxi-rubbish.

* *

THE HOST

APPEARANCE: Humanoid demon with green skin, small horns and red eyes.

WHO IS HE? The Host runs a karaoke bar called Caritas in the Los Angeles underworld. When a demon or human sings, the Host is able to read their aura and give advice or guidance. He is a known associate of the ensouled vampire Angel and his team. Like other members of his clan, the Host can survive having his head removed from his body, as long as his body is not actually destroyed.

PLANET OF ORIGIN: The Host originates from Pylea, a planet with two suns in another dimension. His real name is Krevlorneswath of the Deathwok Clan or Lorne for short. Pylea is connected to the Earth (and other worlds) through portals, which can be opened and closed by a magical chant.

HISTORY: Society on Pylea is medieval with slavery, a ruling priesthood elite and dangerous monsters roaming the countryside. The world contains no music or art – a fact that prompted the music-loving Host to leave. Humans are considered the lowest of the low and referred to as "cows".

LIFESTYLE: An excellent singer, the Host escaped from his own world to live the 'LA dream', baby.

MOST LIKELY TO SAY: "It's called a moment of clarity, my lamb. And you've just had one. Sort of appalling, ain't it? To see just exactly where you've gotten yourself?"

* *

ICE WARRIORS

APPEARANCE: Large, powerful humanoids with green, scaly skin.

WHO ARE THEY? Ice Warriors have visited Earth on several occasions, the first being back in the prehistoric past at the end of the last Ice Age.

Early contacts with them were hostile as they tried to invade Earth using Martian seed pods, among other ruses. The seed pods were designed to absorb the oxygen from the Earth's atmosphere, making the environment more like Mars.

However, later reports indicate they have taken a more peaceful approach to their cosmic neighbours. They have joined the Galactic Federation, even helping the Time Lord known as the Doctor on occasion.

PLANET OF ORIGIN: Mars, under the polar ice caps.

STRENGTHS: They are bullet-proof and can survive in the vacuum of space for short periods.

WEAKNESSES: Ice Warriors are unable to cope with even moderate heat.

WEAPONS: Wrist-mounted sonic guns.

* *

ITALIANS

CATEGORY:
UFO report.

DATE:
18 April 1961.

LOCATION:
Eagle River,
Wisconsin, USA.

WITNESSES:
Farmer Joe
Simonton, aged 60.

APPEARANCE:
The aliens were
dressed in all black
clothes and,
according to Simonton,
"looked just like Italians". The three
beings observed were 1.75 metres tall
with dark hair and an olive complexion.

>>>

MISSION: To get missing ingredients for cooking.

ENCOUNTERED WHEN? Alerted about 11.00 am by a deep, rumbling noise, Simonton left his house to discover a brightly glowing, saucer-shaped craft landing. A hatch opened and the three humanoids emerged. One handed an empty jug to Simonton, apparently asking for it to be filled with water. Simonton obliged and on his return found the men busy cooking food on a grill in the ship.

Simonton handed over the water and the beings gave him three pancakes in return.

AFTER-EFFECTS: Simonton later had the pancakes examined by scientists but they were found to consist of Earthbound ingredients. The only strange thing about them was their complete lack of salt. Eventually, Simonton ate them, but complained that they tasted "like cardboard".

* *

KRYPTONIANS

WHO ARE THEY? Survivors of the destruction of the planet Krypton. On Earth they have superpowers.

WEAKNESSES: Kryptonite.

FAMOUS FACES: Superman (aka Clark Kent) is undoubtedly Krypton's most famous son. Escaping the destruction of Krypton, the infant Kal-El journeyed to Earth where his small rocket crashed. He was found and raised by the childless Kents.

As an adult, he has been working as a reporter for the *Daily Planet* in Metropolis where he met and fell in love with Lois Lane. Superman's crime-fighting career has spanned several decades and seen many highs

and lows, including his apparent death at the hands of Doomsday. Superman's greatest enemy these days is businessman Lex Luthor; other foes include the Toyman, Brainiac, Parasite, Metallo and Bizarro.

For privacy, Superman retreats to his Fortress of Solitude (surely the ultimate boy's clubhouse) hidden away in the snowy wastes of the Antarctic.

Supergirl survived the explosion of Krypton thanks to her presence in the domed Argo City which was cast into space. Her parents later sent her to Earth, where she met her cousin Superman.

SUPERGIRL

LEGION OF SUPERHEROES

WHO ARE THEY? Group of superpowered humanoids from various worlds who fight intergalactic crime in the future.

Members include Superboy, Cosmic Boy, Phantom Girl (who can become immaterial), the telepathic Saturn Girl from Titan, Lightning Lad and the shapechanging Chameleon Boy from the planet Durla.

Perhaps their most memorably named member is Matter-Eater Lad who can eat anything except the deadly compound Magnozite.

* *

LEXX

APPEARANCE: Dragonfly-shaped, sentient spaceship the size of a city.

WHAT IS IT? The Lexx is a fantastically powerful, spacegoing insect which can carry around a crew of smaller beings exactly as a more traditional spaceship would. The Lexx can think for itself, although its intelligence has been likened to that of a loyal but clumsy dog.

HISTORY: The entire Lexx was grown from a small piece of insect matter and was intended to be the flagship of His Shadow's forces.

WHAT HAPPENED? The Lexx is controlled by a special 'key' possessed only by the 'gatekeeper'. When one gatekeeper dies, the key is transferred by touch to the next. Long-time loser Stanley Tweedle just happened to be in the wrong place at the right time and was given sole control over the craft.

MINBARI

APPEARANCE: Humanoid, bald, with a thick, external head bone around their skulls.

WHO ARE THEY? Major spacefaring race. The Minbari society is broken down into three castes – workers, religious and warriors – and ruled by the Grey Council.

HISTORY: Their relations with Earth began on a low point when an Earth ship mistakenly opened fire on its Minbari counterpart. This incident started the Earth-Minbari war, a conflict which cost many lives on both sides and only came to an end during the Battle of the Line. When the Minbari discovered that their souls were being reincarnated into human bodies, they suddenly surrendered.

PLANET OF ORIGIN: Minbar, the seventh planet out from its sun. One quarter of Minbar's surface is taken up by the polar ice cap. The planet's capital city is Yedor and their building style is based heavily on the use of huge, crystal structures.

TRADITIONS: Nafak'cha, Minbari ceremony of rebirth lasting about 24 hours. Each of the participants must reveal a secret that he or she has never told anyone before and must give away something of great personal value.

FAMOUS FACES:

Delenn, the Minbari ambassador to Babylon 5. She underwent a physical transformation to appear more human and later married Commander Sheridan.

Lennier, Delenn's assistant on Babylon 5, secretly in love with her and her most loyal follower.

>>>

WEAKNESSES: Don't take a Minbari out for a drink – alcohol makes them extremely violent.

MOST LIKELY TO SAY: "Life is the universe splitting itself into small pieces in an attempt to understand itself."

"The war is never completely won. There are always new battles to be fought against the darkness. Only the names change."

* *

MON CALAMARI

APPEARANCE: Humanoid fish creatures with large eyes on each side of the face.

WHO ARE THEY? Members of the Rebel Alliance to overthrow the Empire. Mon Calamari are air-breathers but have a liking for water in all forms.

PLANET OF ORIGIN: Mon Calamari (same as species name), a world where much of the surface is water. The Mon Calamari used their great skills as engineers to construct huge, floating cites.

HISTORY: Recently released records reveal the Mon Calamari as long-time members of the old Republic's Senate.

FAMOUS FACES: The best-known individual is Admiral Ackbar of the Rebel Alliance. Ackbar was one of the main battle tacticians during the Rebels' attack on the second Death Star which resulted in the death of Emperor Palpatine. During the Battle of Endor, Admiral Ackbar commanded the rebel forces from *Home One*, his own flagship which had been built on his home world. Ackbar went on to become Commander-in-Chief of military operations for the Rebellion.

ADMIRAL ACKBAR

NORDICS

APPEARANCE: Tall, blond, handsome aliens reported by several witnesses across the Earth who always stress their seemingly 'Scandinavian' looks.

WHO ARE THEY? Rumoured to be a peaceful species interested in helping humanity develop to its full potential.

* *

ROBBY THE ROBOT

WHAT IS HE? Robby was built by the human Dr Morbius using alien Krell technology found on the planet Altair-4 (aka the Forbidden Planet).

STRENGTHS: He can speak 188 languages and can reproduce almost any substance requested using his internal chemical laboratory.

HISTORY: Robby left Altair-4 on Cruiser C-57D just before the planet's destruction. His current whereabouts are unknown.

* *

ROM

WHO IS HE? Cyborg space knight from the planet Galador in the Golden Galaxy. Was transformed by technology to fight evil slug-like creatures called Dire Wraiths.

Rom is armed with a neutraliser which sends the Wraiths on a one-way trip to limbo. He fought Dire Wraiths on Earth alongside heroes such as the X-Men and the Avengers.

SAPPHIRE AND STEEL

WHO ARE THEY? Mysterious beings despatched by an unknown alien authority to deal with problems and dangers caused by the malevolent forces of time.

Sapphire and Steel are two members of a group of 127 'operators and specialists' who are sent to deal with time breaks and corruptions of the continuum.

Sapphire always dresses in blue and has psychic powers. She is 'time sensitive', meaning that she can sense events that have just happened or are about to occur. She can also tell the entire history of any object by scanning it with her hands. More importantly, Sapphire can 'borrow' time, bringing back the recent past.

Her partner Steel dresses in grey, is the logical, cool thinker of the pair and is physically more hardened to his environment.

Both Sapphire and Steel have the power to halt physical movement in other life forms, and to calm them down by a touch. The pair can communicate telepathically with each other.

>>>

MOST LIKELY TO BE INTRODUCED AS: "All irregularities will be handled by the forces controlling each dimension. Transuranic heavy elements may not be used where there is life. Medium atomic weights are available: Gold, Mercury, Copper, Jet, Diamond, Radium, Sapphire, Silver and Steel. Sapphire and Steel have been assigned."

LAST SEEN: Cast adrift in the endless void of the time corridor when they fell into a cleverly concealed trap.

* *

SILVER SURFER

REAL NAME: Norrin Radd.

PLANET OF ORIGIN: Zenn-La, in the Deneb system.

OCCUPATION: Ex-herald of the planet-destroyer Galactus, now galactic wanderer.

APPEARANCE: Beautiful silver being riding on surf board.

LIFESTYLE: Once the Silver Surfer was a normal humanoid on Zenn-La, but when Galactus found the planet and prepared to feed from it, Norrin Radd persuaded him to spare his home world by agreeing to become Galactus's herald and search out other uninhabited worlds for him instead.

Radd was transformed into the Silver Surfer and remained in his role as herald until he rebelled against his master's plans to destroy the Earth. Galactus imprisoned him on Earth for a while as punishment for his betrayal.

LOST LOVE: Shalia Bal, who remained on the Surfer's home world when he left with Galactus.

 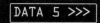

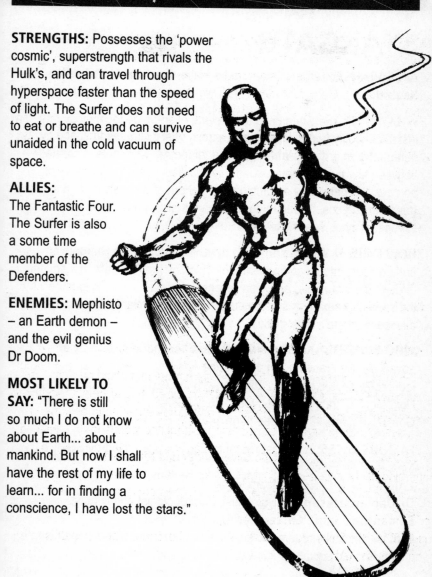

STRENGTHS: Possesses the 'power cosmic', superstrength that rivals the Hulk's, and can travel through hyperspace faster than the speed of light. The Surfer does not need to eat or breathe and can survive unaided in the cold vacuum of space.

ALLIES:
The Fantastic Four. The Surfer is also a some time member of the Defenders.

ENEMIES: Mephisto – an Earth demon – and the evil genius Dr Doom.

MOST LIKELY TO SAY: "There is still so much I do not know about Earth... about mankind. But now I shall have the rest of my life to learn... for in finding a conscience, I have lost the stars."

STARGATE

APPEARANCE: Large, circular portal made of an alien metal called Naquada.

WHAT IS IT? The Stargate is an ancient, alien-made technology that can instantaneously transport a person across vast distances in space by generating an artificial wormhole. The temporary wormhole is created between any two Stargates when one Stargate 'dials' the address of another. Stargates use a combination of 6 out of a possible of 38 symbols (representing constellations) to locate another Stargate, then use a final seventh symbol, specific to each Stargate, to identify its point of origin.

HOW DOES IT WORK? Anything travelling through the Stargate is broken down into its component molecules by the first gate, transmitted through the wormhole, and then reconstituted (i.e. put back together) by the second Stargate at the destination. Many travellers have found that this leaves them a little giddy.

WHO BUILT IT? The Stargates scattered around were built by an advanced alien race known only as the Ancients. They formed a group of four highly advanced races together with the Asgard, the Furlings and the Nox. Much of their advanced technology has been stolen by the the Goa'uld, a parasite race (see page 148).

FAMOUS FACES: A Stargate local to Earth is often used by SG-1, a top-secret Air Force team.
Colonel Jack O'Neill – team leader.
Dr Daniel Jackson – Egyptologist, anthropologist and linguist.
Samantha "Sam" Carter – astrophysicist.
Teal'c – originally ordered to kill the SG-1 team, but abandoned his role in Goa'uld society to join with them instead.

TAUNTAUNS

WHAT ARE THEY? Resembling a cross between a horse and a kangaroo, Tauntauns were used by the Rebel Alliance on the ice planet of Hoth. They are noted for their strong smell, both inside and out.

* *

TELETUBBIES

WHO ARE THEY? Po (who is red in colour and the smallest), Laa-Laa (yellow), Dipsy (green) and Tinky Winky (who is purple and the largest Tubby). Their exact origins are unknown – they may be the result of some human-alien hybrid breeding programme that went horribly wrong.

PLANET OF ORIGIN: Unknown. The Teletubbies now live in Teletubbyland, a strange, green landscape populated by rabbits, a 'baby sun', a windmill and the mysterious voice trumpet. Their home resembles a flying saucer and is kept clean by the Noo-noo, a robotic vacuum cleaner.

CLASSIFIED DATA: Young hatchlings on many worlds throughout the galaxy worship the Teletubbies as gods.

* *

THE TENCTONESE
(AKA NEWCOMERS)

WHO ARE THEY? Humanoid aliens with large, mottled heads.

HISTORY: A quarter of a million Tenctonese were left stranded on Earth when their slave ship crashed in the Mojave Desert. The Newcomers faced racial intolerance as they did their best to settle into Earth society.

THE DOCTORS

TIME LORDS

APPEARANCE: Time Lords can change their appearance and regenerate their bodies after injury or old age wears them out. They have two hearts.

WHO ARE THEY? Members of an ancient race who long ago discovered the secret of time travel. In the early part of their history they were explorers and pioneers, and their society has since become more inward-looking.

Today, they see themselves as the elder statesmen of the universe, living alone and aloof from the younger races, from whom they jealously guard their time technology.

FAMOUS FACES: The Doctor, a free agent who travels thought time and space putting the universe to rights. The Doctor has saved the Earth from alien invasion on countless occasions from would-be conquerors including the Daleks, the Krynoids, the Zygons and the Ice Warriors.

There are also renegade Time Lords like the Doctor's sworn enemy the Master, and the Time Meddler.

PLANET OF ORIGIN: Gallifrey in the Constellation of Kasterborus. The planet is divided into peaceful, highly advanced, domed cities and larger areas of barren wilderness.

STRENGTHS: The technology to travel through time, generally in a TARDIS.

WEAKNESSES: They are a weakening society, no longer really in charge of the galaxy's affairs.

ALIEN ARTEFACTS:
The Hand of Omega – a Time Lord device created by Omega as a stellar manipulator. This was hidden on Earth by the first Doctor　>>>

ALIEN ALLIES

and later retrieved by the seventh Doctor with the help of his assistant Ace. The Hand of Omega made Skaro's sun go supernova, destroying much of the Dalek Empire in the process.

The Key to Time – a powerful relic belonging to 'the Guardians' which can be used to control time itself throughout the universe. It consists of six segments which form a silver cube when assembled. The six segments were last located by the Doctor and his assistant Romana at the bidding of the White Guardian to stop the plans of his evil counterpart, the Black Guardian.

ENEMIES: Sontarans, Daleks, any of the younger races envious of their great powers. In their ancient past, the Time Lords fought a war against a race of great vampires.

ALLIES: None – they believe they are too powerful to need any.

* *

T'POL

WHO IS SHE? Sub-Commander T'Pol is the *Enterprise*'s Science Officer and First Officer. Before Captain Kirk commanded his starship *Enterprise*, another vessel bore the same name. In the 22nd century, pre-Federation, humans had just begun to explore space with help from their newly discovered allies on Vulcan.

WHAT HAPPENED? The Vulcan authorities insisted that T'Pol oversee the first *Enterprise*'s early voyages, refusing to supply star charts unless this demand was met. Later, when faced with a choice between returning to Vulcan for an arranged marriage or staying on the *Enterprise*, T'Pol put her career first. Like the rest of the crew, T'Pol resists the temporal cold war waged by the Suliban and their secret paymaster in the future.

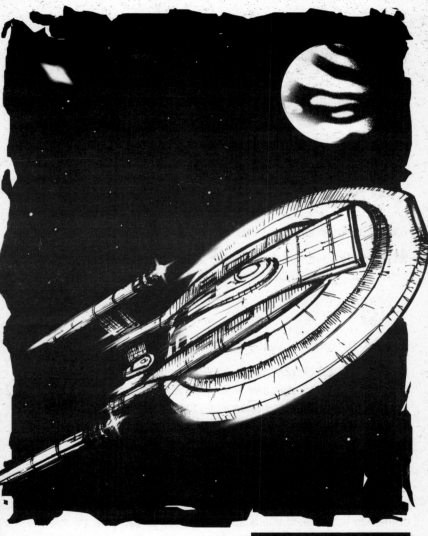

ENTERPRISE

TRILL

WHAT ARE THEY? A 'joined' species, meaning they need a host body to fulfil their potential. Biologically, the Trill are known as symbiotic parasites.

MOST FAMOUS FACE: The late Jadzia Dax, Science Officer on Deep Space Nine. Her Trill symbiont was saved when she was killed and moved into a new host, Ezri Dax.

* *

VENUSIANS

CATEGORY: UFO/contactee report.

WITNESSES: George Adamski, born in Poland in 1891. Adamski was a self-taught man who lectured on universal peace.

APPEARANCE: Humanoid – a form they described to Adamski as being 'universal'.

PLANET OF ORIGIN: Venus – Earth's 'sister' planet.

ENCOUNTERED WHEN? In his book *Flying Saucers have Landed*, Adamski claimed to have met a group of Venusians in the autumn of 1952 in the Californian desert. He described their bell-shaped ship as measuring 13 metres across and being made of some kind of translucent metal. The Venusians communicated with Adamski using both telepathy and sign language.

During a later meeting, the aliens took Adamski on board their ship for a lightning-quick tour of the solar system. During his space travels, Adamski claimed to have met Martians and Saturnians on the surfaces of their own worlds.

Unusually, Adamski was allowed to take several picture of the aliens and their craft. Many of these black and white photographs have since been exposed as fakes.

ALIEN ADVICE: The Venusians were worried about nuclear tests and warned that too many could lead to the extinction of life on Earth.

AFTER-EFFECTS: Adamski became one of the first 'contactees' – people who claim frequent and regular contacts with one particular race of aliens.

* *

VULCANS

APPEARANCE: Humanoid, with pointed ears.

WHO ARE THEY? Founding members of the Federation. For thousands of years Vulcans endured a bloody history until their ancient ancestors finally gained total control over their emotional side and turned to logic as the answer to life's problems. Vulcans have green blood and must return to Vulcan every seven years in a ritual called *pon farr*.

PLANET OF ORIGIN: Vulcan, a hostile desert world with a red sky.

MR SPOCK

STRENGTHS: Intelligent, quick-thinking minds. Can mind-meld with other life forms to gain insights into their thoughts. Can disable opponents with the 'Vulcan nerve pinch' using a small amount of pressure on the victim's neck to render unconsciousness without the need for further violence. **>>>**

FAMOUS FACES: Undoubtedly, Vulcan's best-known export is Mr Spock, who served as First Officer aboard the starship *Enterprise* with the equally legendary Captain James T Kirk. In fact, Spock was only half Vulcan. His mother was a human, Amanda Grayson, and his father the much-respected Ambassador Sarek. In his later years, Spock became an ambassador for the Federation journeying to Romulus in an attempt to unify the Romulan and Vulcan peoples.

Other notable Vulcans include Tuvok, who was Science Officer on the starship *Voyager*, and T'Pol, who served on an earlier *Enterprise* under the command of Captain Jonathan Archer (see page 126).

WEAPONS: A well-raised eyebrow and deadpan witticism. Although Vulcans claim to have suppressed emotions in favour of logic, they are in fact one of the most sarcastic races in the known universe.

MOST LIKELY TO SAY: "That is illogical, Captain." "Fascinating."

LEAST LIKELY TO SAY: "Have you heard the one about the three nuns and the lifeboat…?"

* *

WOOKIEES

APPEARANCE: Tall, powerful, hairy creatures – in the words of Princess Leia, they resemble a "walking carpet". Wookiees stand over two metres tall and are extremely strong.

WHO ARE THEY? Once respected members of the Galactic Republic, Wookiees were forced by the evil Empire to work as slave labour. Wookiees were given back their freedom when the Rebel Alliance finally defeated the Imperial forces.

>>>

 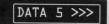

CHEWBACCA

PLANET OF ORIGIN: The jungle world of Kashyyyk.

FAMOUS FACES: The best known Wookiee in the galaxy is Chewbacca, co-pilot and friend of Han Solo, the one-time space pirate and later rebel hero. Chewbacca's fighting skills were particularly effective during the Battle of Endor, where his alliance with the native Ewoks eventually led to the destruction of the Empire's second Death Star.

WEAKNESSES: Wookiees have terrible tempers which can get them into trouble.

WEAPONS: Cutting-edge technology combined with older, more traditional weapons.

ENEMIES: The Empire.

* *

YODA

WHO WAS HE? Jedi master and mentor.

APPEARANCE: Little green goblin.

CAREER: Spent much of his life teaching Jedi Knights across the galaxy. He served the Galactic Republic as one of the 12 members of the Jedi Council. His retirement was spent living the life of a hermit on the swamp planet of Dagobah.

STRENGTHS: Yoda instructed the training and development of Jedi Knights for over 800 years and was at one with the Force. When he needs to be, he can be a powerful warrior with a lightsabre. He trained the young Obi-Wan Kenobi and later, in his final years, Luke Skywalker.

BATTLE TACTICS: Used the Force for knowledge and defence, never attack.

ENEMIES: The dark side of the Force and the Empire.

MOST LIKELY TO SAY: "Try not. Do. Or do not. There is no try."

"A Jedi's strength flows from the Force. But beware the dark side. Anger... fear... aggression. The dark side of the Force are they."

DR ZOIDBERG

APPEARANCE: Stocky, orange doctor with fingers instead of whiskers on his chin and large claws instead of hands.

WHO IS HE? Dr John Zoidberg is from the Decapodian species and is a staff doctor dedicated to healing the sick. His special talents include the ability to squirt ink from his body. His one flaw as a doctor is his complete incompetence.

ENJOYS: Performing delicate surgery while doing stand-up comedy and eating raw garbage.

* *

ZOONIE THE LAZOON

APPEARANCE: Weird but cute. Zoonie resembles a cross between a monkey and a koala bear.

WHO IS HE? Resident pet on board the World Space Patrol's *Fireball XL-5* piloted by Colonel Steve Zodiac. Zoonie is owned by Steve's girlfriend Venus.

```
DATA 5 COMPLETE
```

ALIEN ENEMIES AND AGGRESSORS

From the cold vacuum of space to the destructive inferno of a star's core, there's no escaping the fact that the universe is a very hostile place. There are more natural hazards than you can shake a Tribble at, and the place is crawling with life forms who want nothing more than to kill, exterminate, assimilate, eat, attack, shoot, stab, poison and cook you, while generally saying terrible things about your mother. This data file lets you know just who your enemies are.

>>>

ANDROMEDA STRAIN

APPEARANCE: Err... small.

WHAT WAS IT? Microscopic life form that was brought back from space by the probe *Scope VII*.

A team of four human scientists raced against time to discover what had wiped out almost the entire population of Piedmont, Arizona, USA. Only one old man and a baby remained alive.

* *

BERSERKERS

WHAT ARE THEY? Not an alien life form, but rather the dangerous, space-going legacy created by an ancient race known only as 'the Builders'. Berserkers are huge, sphere-shaped spacecraft programmed to destroy life anywhere they find it in the universe.

APPEARANCE: Floating space fortress.

PLANET OF ORIGIN: The Berserkers were built as weapons of war, but the machines turned on their own creators and wiped them out. They then journeyed out into space and began following their programme to destroy all life.

STRENGTHS: They have the capacity to repair themselves and are fitted with a vast number of advanced weapons, including forms of biological warfare.

WARNING: Although now rare, Berserkers continue to be a danger to planets and property prices thoughout the galaxy.

BLACK OIL

WHAT IS IT? Intelligent, alien life form investigated by Mulder and Scully. The black ooze enters the victim's brain through the nose, eyes or mouth and takes control of the host. Later reports suggest that the oil may actually cause a change in the genetic make-up of its host.

WHAT HAPPENED? Mulder and Doggett investigated a case where the Black Oil had taken over workers on an oil rig in the Gulf of Mexico. Rather than be captured as evidence, the controlling oil made the men destroy their own rig.

* *

BLOB

SPECIES: Unknown. Probably not sentient. The Blob may be an alien super-virus that has achieved an enormous reproductive rate.

APPEARANCE: Huge mass of jelly that grows by absorbing other life forms.

HOW DID IT REACH EARTH? The Blob arrived inside a meteor that crashed in a forest near a small Pennsylvania town.

STRENGTHS: The Blob cannot be harmed by bullets, chemicals, electricity, gas, fire or witty remarks. It can absorb and therefore feed on almost all living matter.

WEAKNESSES: Its one weakness is extreme cold, which reduces the Blob's mobility and can eventually freeze it solid.

LEAST LIKELY TO SAY: Anything.

BORG

WHO ARE THEY? One of the most dangerous and aggressive races in the universe. The Borg 'assimilate' other species, forcing them to become part of the Borg collective. Their spacecraft are huge cubes with complex, hive-like interiors.

PLANET OF ORIGIN: Unknown. The Borg have a huge collective made up of many worlds in the Delta Quadrant, as recorded by the crew of the starship *Voyager*.

HISTORY: Among other targets, the Borg destroyed the New Providence colony at Jouret IV. This incident was followed by the Borg abduction of Captain Picard from the starship *Enterprise* and shortly afterwards the disastrous Battle at Wolf 359.

Wolf 359 was one of the worst defeats ever inflicted on the Federation, as the fleet made its stand against a Borg cube heading for Earth. Altogether 39 starships were destroyed with the loss of 11,000 Starfleet personnel.

STRENGTHS: Highly advanced technology and weapons, which have often been taken from races and cultures that they have assimilated.

Their command structure is spread evenly throughout their space-going cubes, which means that there is no one bridge or command centre vulnerable in battle. A Borg cube can remain fully active and engaged in combat with up to 20 per cent of its structure destroyed. Anything that one Borg learns, they all know instantly.

WEAKNESSES: Various – thanks to the nature of their collective mind.

The Borg cube en route to Earth was destroyed when a rescued Captain Picard was able to link with the Borg collective mind and issue an order to put them to sleep.

FAMOUS FACE: Seven of Nine, who was rescued from the Borg by the starship *Voyager*. Seven of Nine was formerly named Annika Hansen. Annika's parents were last seen leaving a remote outpost in the Omega sector, headed towards the Delta Quadrant in a small space vessel, *The Raven*. It is likely that the Hansen family were the first humans ever assimilated by the Borg.

MOST LIKELY TO SAY: "We are the Borg. You will be assimilated. Resistance is futile. Your biological and technological distinctiveness will be added to our own."

* *

CARDASSIANS

WHO ARE THEY? Grey-skinned humanoids with neck and face ridges, particularly noted for their cunning. Known throughout the galaxy for their lies and deception. The Obsidian Order, which is the Cardassian secret service, is one of the most feared in all the cosmos.

PLANET OF ORIGIN: Cardassia Prime in the Alpha Quadrant of the Milky Way galaxy. The Cardassians once occupied Bajor and constructed Deep Space Nine, then known as Terok Nor, using Bajorian slave labour.

HISTORY: The Cardassian Empire was at war with the Federation for a time. Ambassador Sarek attempted to negotiate a peaceful settlement, but was publicly opposed by his son Spock.

FAMOUS FACE: Garak, Deep Space Nine's 'simple tailor'.

BIGGEST MISTAKE EVER: They entered into an alliance with the evil Dominion (see page 87), hoping to defeat their enemies in the Federation. However, the Dominion was using their new allies for military advantage. Eventually, the Cardassians rebelled but at terrible cost. They suffered heavy casualties in the war and Cardassia Prime was left in ruins.

CHIGS

APPEARANCE: Humanoids with neck gills and black eyes. They usually wear protective armour.

WHO ARE THEY? Mysterious alien race (nicknamed Chigs by humans) who attacked Earth's colonies in the year 2063, plunging humanity into an unexpected and unwanted war.

After decades of exploring space and encountering no alien life, humans had come to believe that they were alone in the universe. Having established a new colony on Tellus, 16 light years away, humanity was shocked when a devastating alien attack obliterated it.

US Marine Corps Space Cavalry were quickly moved into the front-line of the conflict and rose to the challenge 'above and beyond' the call of duty.

STRENGTHS: Chig technology is centuries ahead of Earth's and includes spacecraft invisible to radar.

WEAKNESSES: Their chemical make-up means that water has a deadly, corrosive effect on their bodies.

CLASSIFIED DATA: Chigs are rumoured to have visited Earth in the distant past, and had contact with the Native American peoples.

* *

CYBERMEN

APPEARANCE: Silver-suited humanoids.

WHO ARE THEY? The Cybermen were once human but gradually replaced parts of their bodies with metals and artificial materials until they became emotionless creatures of war.

PLANET OF ORIGIN: Mondas, Earth's twin planet, was their original home. After Mondas was destroyed during an attempt to invade Earth, they later settled on Telos. In recent times, they have become homeless space wanderers just desperate to survive.

STRENGTHS: They have the physical force of ten men and can live in a vacuum.

>>>

WEAKNESSES: Vulnerable to the metal gold, particularly in the form of gold dust which clogs their internal systems.

BATTLE TACTICS: Often attempt a 'quiet' invasion – using Cybermats or a virus – rather than relying on military force.

WEAPONS: Cybermats – small, silver creatures used as front line of attack.

ENEMIES: The Cyberwars with Earth nearly led to the Cybermen's extinction. The Time Lord known as the Doctor remains their most hated enemy, having defeated them on nearly a dozen occasions.

ALLIES: None.

MOST LIKELY TO SAY: "You will become like us."

* *

CYLONS

APPEARANCE: Silver robots with red eye beams and metallic voices.

WHO ARE THEY? Deadly enemies of humankind, Cylons have been waging a war to exterminate humans from the universe for over a thousand years. It is rumoured that the original Cylons were reptiles, but they have since died out, leaving their robots to carry on their crusade.

The Cylons succeeded in destroying much of humanity, sending the few survivors off on a desperate quest across deep space looking for a lost 13th colony called Earth. The flagship of the survivors' fleet was *Battlestar Galactica*, led by Commander Adama.

PLANET OF ORIGIN: Located in a distant galaxy.

STRENGTHS: There appear to be millions of Cylons, all with absolutely nothing better to do than chase humans across the stars.

WEAKNESSES: Stupid. Very, very stupid. Cylons are slow-witted, slow-moving and, above all else, lousy shots with a laser pistol.

Their well-spoken commander, known as Imperious Leader, hatched one misguided plan after another, in an attempt to catch *Galactica*. They all failed.

BATTLE TACTICS: The Cylon's pursuit of humanity was relentless, lasting the entire 30 years it took the *Galactica* to reach Earth. They arrived in 1980. Realising that Earth's technology and weapons were not advanced enough to defeat the following Cylons, Commander Adama tried to ensure that the Cylons did not discover the position of the planet. While the fleet led the Cylons away from Earth, a team from *Galactica* attempted to advance the planet's technology.

ALLIES: Humankind was betrayed by Count Baltar, a nasty, snivelling piece of work.

WARNING: Travellers coming into contact with Cylons are asked on no account to reveal the location of the planet Earth.

* *

DALEKS

APPEARANCE: Gliding pepperpots.

WHO ARE THEY? They're nasty. Along with the Borg and the Thing, they are one of the most feared and aggressive life forms in the known universe. The warlike Daleks have invaded countless star systems in their quest for total galactic domination.

The Daleks were created by the evil scientist Davros during the centuries-long war between the Kaleds and the Thals. The Kaleds had become genetically polluted and the Dalek creatures inside the machines are their mutated remains.

>>>

YOU WILL OBEY!

PLANET OF ORIGIN: Skaro, the 12th planet in its system.

STRENGTHS: They never, ever give up.

WEAKNESSES: One word – stairs.

BATTLE TACTICS: In recent years, the once mighty Dalek Empire has collapsed into in-fighting between the Imperial Daleks and a separate faction led by their creator, Davros. As long as the Daleks keep battling each other, galactic supremacy will continue to escape them.

WEAPONS: Their famous exterminators.

ENEMIES: Most other races in the galaxy, especially the Movellans – a race of humanoid robots.

ALLIES: Have used Ogrons, strong, ape-like beings, as their servants and foot soldiers. Have also been known to work with the rogue Time Lord the Master, although their last dealings with him did not end happily.

MOST LIKELY TO SAY: "Exterminate!"

LEAST LIKELY TO SAY: "What are you doing Friday night?"

* *

DRAKH

WHO ARE THEY? Dark servants of the Shadows. Although their former masters have departed beyond the galactic rim, their servants remain to threaten interstellar peace.

BATTLE TACTICS: The Drakh recently manipulated members of the Earth Alliance into performing a devastating attack on the Centauri home world of Centauri Prime.

GALACTUS

APPEARANCE: Ten-metre tall humanoid weighing nearly 20 tonnes.

PLANET OF ORIGIN: The planet Taa in the universe which existed before the last Big Bang.

OCCUPATION: Destroyer of worlds.

LIFESTYLE: Galactus travels the universe looking for worlds to drain of energy and destroy. He has made several attempts to use the Earth to feed his hunger, but has been stopped repeatedly by the Fantastic Four.

STRENGTHS: He is an incredibly powerful being and can tap into cosmic forces to shape them to his own ends.

WEAKNESSES: The Ultimate Nullifier – an alien device which can destroy even him.

BATTLE TACTICS: Galactus uses elemental converters to dehydrate a planet's oceans, then his cosmic rays destroy all the cities before his planet-encircling ray reduces the entire globe to a lifeless, empty husk. Finally, he drains the planet's fiery core, leaving nothing behind but a few floating fragments in the place where there was once a thriving world.

ENEMIES: He represents a huge menace to all space-going races and planets where there is intelligent life. He recently destroyed the throne world of the Skrulls, throwing their entire empire into disarray.

MOST LIKELY TO SAY: "This planet contains the energy I need to sustain me! I shall absorb it at will... as I have done for ages, for countless galaxies throughout the cosmos!"

WARNING: Travellers of all species are advised to leave any solar system in which Galactus appears.

THE GOA'ULD

APPEARANCE: Human – see below.

WHO ARE THEY? Snake-like parasites about 30 centimetres long.

WHAT DO THEY DO? Like the Trill (page 128), they are a symbiotic race. They enter their (unwilling) host and take up residence between the brain stem and spinal cord. The giveaway clue that someone has been taken over by the Goa'uld is the small, vertical scar left on the victim's upper back, made as the Goa'uld enters its host's body for the first time.

Other indications include: the victim's eyes may glow; they speak in a spooky voice, lower than usual; they try and take over your planet.

HEALTH NOTE: A matured Goa'uld is able to transfer between hosts by crawling into the new host's mouth. (Ugh!) A full medical scan is recommended for travellers who think that they or a relative may have been in contact with this race.

LIFESTYLE: Outside of the protective body of a host, the Goa'uld are weak, small and puny. However, use of their (stolen) advanced technology (including Stargates) and moving from host body to host body mean that these creatures can sometimes live for thousands of years.

* *

THE HIDDEN

WHAT ARE THEY? Reptilian parasites that enter the human host through the mouth. Once inside, the Hidden can control its host's actions. Often it enjoys making them murder and kill. One was hunted down in Los Angeles by FBI agent Lloyd Gallagher and detective Tom Beck.

THE INVISIBLES

WHAT ARE THEY? Parasites that attach themselves to the spinal cords of humans and are then able to control their hosts. The super-intelligent slugs attempted to take over Earth after their journey here from the Outer Limits of deep space.

* *

JABBA THE HUTT

WHO WAS HE? Crimelord of Tatooine. Jabba had a massive, bulbous, slug-like body and a laugh like a drain. His father was the crimelord Zorba the Hutt. Jabba lived to be many hundreds of years old and his vast array of illegal activities included blackmail, extortion, running pod races, smuggling, protection rackets and murder.

HOW DID HE DIE? He met his end at the hands of his new 'slave girl' Princess Leia when he attempted to put Luke Skywalker and Han Solo to death.

JEM'HADAR

WHO ARE THEY? Specially bred soldiers born to serve the Founders of the Dominion (see page 87). A strong and dangerous warrior race, they have a hatred of all races other than the Founders built into their DNA. The Jem'Hadar are chemically dependant on a substance called Ketracel White which insures their total obedience and loyalty to the Dominion at all times.

MOST LIKELY TO SAY: "I am First Omet'iklan and I am dead. As of this moment, we are all dead. We go into battle to reclaim our lives. This we do gladly, for we are Jem'Hadar. Remember, victory is life."

* *

KLINGONS

APPEARANCE: Powerful humanoids with a ridge of bone running up the centre of their foreheads.

WHO ARE THEY? Warlike enemies of the Federation who were forced to negotiate for peace after their moon Praxis exploded in 2293.

Their society revolves around their codes of honour, loyalty and courage. As a race they are quick to anger and slow to forgive.

PLANET OF ORIGIN: Qo'noS (pronounced 'Kronos'). The Klingon Empire was founded by Kahless the Unforgettable 1500 years ago. At its peak, it included 750 worlds.

Klingons first encountered humans when a Klingon warrior crash-landed on Earth in the 22nd century. The warrior was returned to Klingon space by the first starship *Enterprise* under the command of Captain Jonathan Archer.

STRENGTHS: Their bloody-mindedness and their bravery in battle. Klingons posses a back-up nervous system which can keep them alive even after a serious injury. Klingons have no tear ducts and so cannot cry.

WEAKNESSES: Their lust for battle often stops them seeing the bigger picture. They are obsessed with family and traditional rituals to the exclusion of much else.

Pet hates: Tribbles – who dislike Klingons intensely.

FAMOUS FACE: Worf, third in command of the starship *Enterprise* under Captain Picard. Worf was born on Qo'noS in 2340, but was raised by humans after a Romulan attack killed his family. >>>

Some records indicate that Worf was the first Klingon ever to join Starfleet. Spends much of his time and energy on needless shouting.

BATTLE TACTICS: Relentless, sledgehammer tactics. Klingons live to fight and will fight to the last Klingon. For them to die in battle is the most glorious exit of all. They are not adverse to stealing other races' technology.

WEAPONS: Disruptors – weapons that scramble the victim's internal organs and are outlawed by the Federation. Agonisers – devices with the sole purpose of inflicting pain.

ALIEN ARTEFACT: The Sword of Kahless is a legendary Klingon relic which stories say will help reunite the Klingon Empire. Rumoured to have been sighted in the Gamma Quadrant.

ENEMIES: The Dominion – who manipulated the Klingon Empire into briefly renewing hostilities with the Federation.

ALLIES: Since the last days of Captain Kirk's active service, the Klingons and the Federation have been uneasy allies. Their pact is now cemented as they battle their joint enemy, the Dominion.

MOST LIKELY TO SAY: "Today is a good day to die!"

* *

KRANG

WHO IS HE? Pink, brain-like blob from another dimension. Teamed up with the ruthless Shredder to confront the Teenage Mutant Ninja Turtles on numerous occasions, but his ambitious plans have always met with defeat and disaster.

KREE

APPEARANCE: Blue-skinned and pink-skinned humanoids.

WHO ARE THEY? Creators of a star empire that extends over nearly a thousand worlds.

>>>

1970

1967

WHO'S IN CHARGE: The Supreme Intelligence. The ruler of the Kree Empire is a vast, organic computer which uses the preserved brains of their greatest scientists and thinkers.

PLANET OF ORIGIN: Hala, Pama system, in the Greater Magellanic Cloud.

STRENGTHS: On Earth they have twice the strength of humans. The development of their muscles is due to the greater gravity on their home world. Their technology is hundreds of years in advance of Earth's.

WEAKNESSES: As a race their empire faces an uncertain future – the most likely prospect is slow decay.

FAMOUS FACES: Captain Marvel, a one-time Kree war hero who defected to the side of humanity.

ENEMIES: The Skrulls.

* *

KYBEN

WHO ARE THEY? Race of aliens from the Outer Limits of space. The Kyben conquered Earth in the year 2964 with a war that lasted only 19 days. However, their victory was a hollow one, for every human on the planet had suddenly vanished, leaving only a deadly, radioactive plague infesting the surface.

WHAT HAPPENED? Humans had cheated the Kyben by electronically transcribing every individual on to a thin strand of gold-copper alloy secretly kept safe in the possession of Trent (aka the Demon with a Glass Hand). Trent awoke with no memory of these events in 1964 and found himself under attack by Kyben travelling back into Earth's past using a 'time mirror'.

MANDRAGORA HELIX

WHAT IS IT? Bodiless, energy life form, one of a number of helix intelligences which lives in the time vortex. They can manipulate and transform energy into matter. The fourth Doctor and Sarah Jane Smith accidentally transported it to 15th century Italy where it attempted to change Earth history.

* *

MARVIN THE MARTIAN
(AKA COMMANDER X-2)

OCCUPATION: Space explorer and fearless warrior

APPEARANCE: Small, ant-like being wearing a Roman-style helmet and skirt.

LIFESTYLE: Marvin has visited the Earth's moon, where he met Bugs Bunny. Marvin's mission was to destroy the Earth, using his Aludium Q36 Explosive Space Modulator, because it "obstructed my view of Venus". Marvin was accompanied by his faithful Martian hound, K-9.

>>>

Later, he voyaged to Planet X where he encountered Duck Dodgers in the 24½ century, and his assistant space cadet Porky Pig. Earth and Mars fought a vicious battle for the new world, reducing the planet itself to almost nothing.

SPACECRAFT: The *Martian Maggot*.

WEAPONS: A-1 disintegrating pistol.

* *

THE MEKON

APPEARANCE: Green, dome-headed humanoid with enormous brain power.

WHO IS HE? The Mekon moves around on his floating hoverchair powered by the might of his mind alone.

PLANET OF ORIGIN: Venus. Member of the Treen race, native to the northern half of the planet. The Mekon is rumoured to be the result of genetic experiments aimed at increasing the Treen's intelligence and providing them with a leader.

WHAT HAPPENED? The Mekon and his Treen followers attempted to conquer the rest of Venus; however, the Therons of southern Venus had formed an alliance with Earth and the Mekon's forces were defeated, thanks to Earth pilot Dan Dare.

The Mekon was exiled from Venus and became a lonely figure wandering the spaceways. He still plots revenge on Dan Dare.

MOST LIKELY TO SAY: "We meet again, Colonel Dare! This is your master – the mighty Mekon of Mekonta!"

METAL MASTER

WHO IS HE? Humanoid from Astra, a planet where all natives have the ability to shape and control metal by willpower alone. The Metal Master once menaced the Earth, but was defeated by the Hulk very early in the latter's colourful career.

* *

OGRONS

WHO ARE THEY? A race of ape-like beings used as foot soldiers and slaves by the Daleks. Usually armed with neuronic stun guns

* *

THE OLD ONES

APPEARANCE: OK, you asked. Few people have ever seen an Old One and lived to tell the tale, but those who have managed to escape in time describe them as being nearly three metres long with barrel-shaped bodies. They have greyish, tough skin and a five-metre wingspan. Around the centre of their body are five stalks that branch into smaller tentacles, giving each stalk a total of 25 tentacles. Each of these tentacles extends to almost one metre. Their heads are yellowish and starfish-shaped, with a glassy, red-irised eye on the end of each point. Extending from the head is what looks like a sack of sharp, white teeth.

WHO ARE THEY? A very ancient race of elder gods.

HISTORY: The Old Ones first came to Earth over two billion years ago, before humans, before dinosaurs, before life itself. They travelled through deep space without the need of spacecraft, protected >>>

from the void by their thick skins. They founded mighty cities on the Earth's ocean floors, protected from the great pressures there by the same body strength that made their journey through space possible.

They endured several wars with other races from the stars. Although hideous in appearance, the Old Ones are fantastically intelligent and also cultured. They left behind many amazingly detailed wall murals carved into the walls of their underwater cities.

LIFESTYLE: They reproduce by means of spores; so Saturday night dating is not a big thing in their society.

WHAT HAPPENED? The Old Ones are rumoured to be lying in a deathless sleep, awaiting the day when they might return to reclaim the Earth. (See also Cthulhu, page 220.)

ENCOUNTERED BY: Professor Lake and his team during an expedition to the Mountains of Madness in the Antarctic. The Professor discovered what he thought were dead bodies of the Old Ones frozen in a cave. However, even a frozen hibernation of over 56 million years wasn't enough to kill the creatures; they promptly woke up and slaughtered the entire expedition.

* *

RED WEED

WHAT WAS IT? Martian vegetation brought by the invaders (either accidentally or as part of their invasion plan) during the War of the Worlds incident. The fast-growing weed thrived on water and covered the major cities of the world at an alarming rate, turning the Earth's landscape the crimson red of Mars.

ROMULANS

APPEARANCE: Their pointed ears and high cheekbones make them resemble their relatives, the Vulcans. Romulans are descended from a rebel Vulcan colony who refused to suppress their emotions.

WHO ARE THEY? They were first encountered by Starfleet in the middle of the 22nd century, leading to a major space battle between the two forces. After the Romulan War with Earth ended in 2160, an area known as the Neutral Zone was set up to act as a buffer between the space-going powers. The Neutral Zone is one light year wide and was totally unbreached for over ahundred years until 2266.

The current accord between the Federation the Romulans is the treaty of Algeron, which maintains the Neutral Zone and thereby Romulan isolation.

PLANET OF ORIGIN: Romulus and Remus.

RULING BODY: Romulan Senate.

STRENGTHS: Their ships (classed as War Birds and Birds-of-Prey) are equipped with a cloaking device which can render them invisible. They share this technology with the Klingon Empire.

WEAKNESSES: Arrogance.

BATTLE TACTICS: All or nothing.

 >>>

ROMULAN

WEAPONS: Disruptors – weapons that scramble the victim's internal organs. These are outlawed by the Federation.

ENEMIES: Cold war enemies of the Federation. Rumours also suggest that the Romulans have recently engaged in a long, military battle against another space power – quite possibly the Borg.

CLASSIFIED DATA: The Tal Shiar is the much-feared intelligence wing of the Romulan Empire. This secret service spends much time attempting to stop the activities of an underground movement of Romulans who want to see their race reunited with their long-lost cousins on Vulcan.

* *

SHADOWS

APPEARANCE: Black spiders.

WHO ARE THEY? One of the galaxy's most ancient and powerful races. 'Shadows' is the human name for them. Their real name is 10,000 letters long and totally unpronounceable.

PLANET OF ORIGIN: Z'ha'dum, a barren, red world on the edge of known space.

STRENGTHS: Hugely advanced organic technology. Telepathic ability to affect some human minds. Ability to turn invisible.

WEAKNESSES: Their spider-like spaceships are vulnerable to disruption from telepaths.

BATTLE TACTICS: The Shadows emerge from the universe's dark corners every 1000 years or so to spread chaos and destruction across the galaxy. Their intention is to "kick over all the anthills" of the lesser races, believing that only war and conflict can lead to growth.   >>>

ANCIENT EVIL

WHAT HAPPENED? The Shadows were awakened from their 1000-year sleep by the arrival of the Earth ship *Icarus* on Z'ha'dum.

WEAPONS: Numerous and deadly. One of their weapons can split open the entire crust of a planet, turning it inside out.

ENEMIES: The Vorlons – their foes in the Great War.

ALLIES: Although the Shadows have now passed beyond the rim with the Vorlons, their technology and their former servants, the Drakh, still remain to cause problems for the personnel of Babylon 5.

* *

SONTARANS

APPEARANCE: All Sontarans look similar because they are a race of sexless clone warriors.

WHO ARE THEY? At one point, the Sontarans dared to attempt an invasion of Gallifrey, the home world of the Time Lords. They were defeated by the Doctor and his assistant Leela.

FAMOUS FACE: Linx, Sontaran warrior who crash-landed in England in the Middle Ages. His scheme to kidnap scientists from the 20th century was defeated by the third Doctor and Sarah Jane Smith.

STRENGTHS: The Sontaran army of green-blooded clones numbers hundreds of millions.

WEAKNESSES: Physically very powerful, their only real weakness is a vent on the back of their neck through which they recharge themselves, feeding on pure energy.

BATTLE TACTICS: They are very methodical and investigate their enemies, gathering data by performing experiments on captured test subjects before they begin any military campaign.

WEAPONS: Numerous and deadly. Sontarans usually carry wand-like guns that can kill or stun. The army has photonic missiles.

ENEMIES: Engaged in a long-running war with a race called the Rutans who resemble large, green blobs with tentacles.

* *

SPACE PHANTOM

APPEARANCE: Humanoid.

WHO IS HE? Sole survivor of the planet Phantus, now lost in limbo thanks to time travel wars which confused the time stream. Came to Earth and fought the superhero group, the Avengers. His superpower enabled him to take the form of any person, who was banished to limbo while the Space Phantom wore their shape.

* *

SUTEKH

WHO WAS HE? Last survivor of the powerful race known as the Osirans, who were worshipped as gods by the Ancient Egyptians. Sutekh's full title was Sutekh the Destroyer.

WHAT HAPPENED? Sutekh committed terrible crimes and was imprisoned in an ancient pyramid as punishment. By mind-controlling a number of humans in 1911, Sutekh attempted to free himself from his eternal prison, but his escape plan was foiled by the fourth Doctor and Sarah Jane Smith, sending Sutekh to his death at the end of time.

THOLIANS

WHO ARE THEY? Little is known of this mysterious race because humans have rarely travelled into their space empire and survived. They are a secretive race with a crystalline body structure.

WEAPONS: Their spaceships build giant webs in space to trap and defeat their enemies.

* *

TRIPODS

WHO ARE THEY? One of the few races to succeed, at least in part, in conquering Earth. They were the creation of mysterious aliens known only as the Masters who came to Earth to live in the City of Gold and Lead.

APPEARANCE: Tall, three-legged, alien machines.

PLANET OF ORIGIN: The planet Trion.

WHAT HAPPENED? Under a system of mind control called 'capping' human society returned to a medieval existence. The Tripods ruled mankind for a hundred years and planned to change the Earth's atmosphere to one more suited to themselves.

* *

WAR OF THE WORLDS

WHAT WAS IT? Attempted invasion of Earth by Martians. The Martians launched themselves at a totally unprepared world, arriving in huge, silver cylinders.

WHAT HAPPENED? Of all the alien invasion attempts of the Earth

detailed in this volume, the Martian invasion was one of the most ruthless and destructive, causing entire populations to go on the run or face certain death. Under the crushing Martian onslaught, human society collapsed, leaving pockets of survivors driven half mad with fear and hunger.

APPEARANCE: Described as having "huge round heads about four feet in diameter. In a group round the mouth were 16 slender, almost whip-like tentacles. The lipless brim of its mouth quivered and panted and dropped saliva."

BATTLE TACTICS: The aliens used the cover of their pit to build a tripod fighting machine and, as other cylinders began to fall to Earth all over the world, set about their systematic destruction of humankind.

WEAPONS: Tripod fighting machines, 'Black Smoke' and deadly heat-rays.

>>>

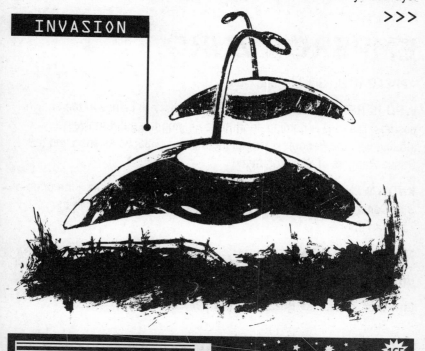

INVASION

WHY DID THEY INVADE? During the invasion it was discovered that the Martians themselves were mostly brain matter, and fed on injections of blood from other living things. To them, humans were little more than livestock to be farmed for slaughter.

HOW WERE THEY DEFEATED? Humanity could do nothing to repel its conquerors. However, the Martians fell victim to Earth bacteria against which they had no defence. They were "Slain by the humblest things that God, in his wisdom, has put upon this Earth."

NOT TO BE CONFUSED WITH: Mars is also home to more peaceful races such as the Ice Warriors. It now seems likely that this 'War of the Worlds' invasion attempt was the last throw of the dice for a dying and desperate species.

* *

EMPEROR ZURG

APPEARANCE: Big, bad and blue.

WHO IS HE? Emperor Zurg is one of the most evil beings in the known cosmos. His goal is nothing short of destroying the entire universe, starting with the freedom-loving planets of the Galactic Alliance and the Space Rangers of Star Command.

KNOWN ENEMIES: Buzz "to infinity and beyond" Lightyear – the pride of Star Command, and Princess Mira Nova – the all-action heir to the Tangean throne.

MEMORABLE QUOTE:

Buzz Lightyear: "You killed my father!"

Emperor Zurg: "No, Buzz, I am your father."

ZURG

DATA 6 COMPLETE

>>> LOADING

ALIEN ODDBALLS

There is a saying on Sirius IV that there's "nowt as strange as folk". It expresses much the same sentiment as the well-known bumper sticker from Rigel VI: "There's an awful lot of weirdos out there." Both statements are certainly true of the following collection of intergalactic eccentrics, weirdos and just plain loonies. These, then, are the oddballs of the cosmos, everything from little self-replicating balls of fur called Tribbles, to the giant Sandworms of Dune.

>>>

ANTHEANS

WHO ARE THEY? Dead or dying species from the planet Anthean.

NAME: Thomas Jerome Newton (aka the Man Who Fell to Earth).

APPEARANCE: Thin humanoid. Wears contact lenses to hide his alien eyes.

OCCUPATION: Newton was sent to Earth in his race's last working spacecraft on a mission to save his species from extinction.

LIFESTYLE: When Newton first arrived, he set about his mission with zeal, registering nine alien inventions that will make him and his company 300 million dollars in the next three years.

He intended to use his fortune to build a spacecraft capable of returning to his home world with the water and resources needed to revitalise his people and their barren planet. However, gradually, Newton lost sight of his goal. He became addicted to television and ran his company, World Enterprises, as a recluse.

ENEMIES: Rival Earth businessmen who don't like the success of World Enterprises.

MOST LIKELY TO SAY: "We face extinction. We have almost no water, no fuel, no natural resources. We have feeble solar power – feeble because we are so far from the sun... There are fewer than 300 Antheans alive."

OUTLOOK: Bleak. His company eventually went bankrupt. Newton was left totally alone and wandering the Earth, knowing that he had left his family and people to face a slow but certain death.

* *

BABYLON 5

WHAT IS IT? Located in neutral space, Babylon 5 is a home or port of call for many alien races. However, because "sooner or later everybody comes to Babylon 5", the informed galactic traveller would be wise to make note of the following:

WHO ARE THEY?

The Drazi – a small-minded and aggressive species. Every five years all the members divide into two groups – the green and the purple – and fight each other. The winning group gets to rule the losers.

The Markab – victims of a galactic plague. Their dead world has now been ransacked by other races.

The Pak'ma'ra – a race of intelligent scavengers who eat the flesh of the dead. (Note: Don't invite them to family funerals.)

Soul Hunters – a religious order. They are drawn to the deaths of famous "leaders, thinkers, poets, dreamers, and blessed lunatics" in an effort to capture and thereby 'save' their souls.

The Vinzini – eight-legged insectoids. According to Londo Mollari, they are terrible at card games.

Other races present on Babylon 5 include the Narn, the Minbari, the Vorlons and many lesser species such as the Abbai, the Brakiri, the Hyach, the Gaim, the Ipsha, the Llort and the Vree.

BANTHAS

WHAT ARE THEY? Large, stocky creatures with thick, dirty fur standing two or three metres tall. The males have a pair of long, spiralling horns. Native to the deserts of Tatooine, these slow-moving animals are used as beasts of burden by the Sand People (see page 193).

* *

CANTINA ALIENS

WHERE ARE THEY? In the Mos Eisley spaceport on Tatooine, described by Ben Kenobi as "a hive of scum and villainy". It is home to an eye-opening number of weird life forms. Information on these species is largely based on rumour and hearsay.

WHO ARE THEY? They include:

Arcona – humanoid snakes with flat heads from the planet Cona.
Hammerhead – the nickname of a strange-shaped alien, actually an Ithorian called Momaw Nadon. Ithorians are primarily peaceful space merchants from the tropical world of Ithor.
Rodians – the best-known member of this species was Greedo, a bounty hunter used by Jabba the Hutt to track down Han Solo. Greedo made the mistake of finding him and died shortly afterwards.

* *

CENTAURI

APPEARANCE: Humanoids. The females shave their heads, while the males have big, big hair, its size depending on their rank.

WHO ARE THEY? A proud, spacefaring race whose empire has seen better days.

PLANET OF ORIGIN: Centauri Prime, a world 75 light years from Babylon 5.

FAMOUS FACE: Londo Mollari was the Centauri Ambassador to Babylon 5. Dreaming of a way to restore his people to their former glory, Londo entered into a deal with Morden, an agent of the Shadows.

LONDO MOLLARI

At first the destruction of various Narn outposts meant that the Ambassador's star was seen to be rising in the Emperor's court back home. However, eventually, after the destruction and conquest of the Narn home world, even Londo realised the price was too high. He cut his ties to Morden and the Shadows, and joined the battle against the darkness.

MOST LIKELY TO SAY: "Do you really want to know what I want? I want to see the Centauri stretch forth their hand again and command the stars. I want a rebirth of glory – a renaissance of power. I want to stop running through my life like a man late for an appointment, afraid to look back or look forward. I want us to be what we used to be. I want... I want it all back the way it was." – Londo Mollari.

WEAKNESSES: Centauri often dream of how they are going to die – a vision that can then haunt them for years. Londo knows that he will die with the Narn hands of G'Kar tightening around his neck.

>>>

ENEMIES: The Narn and, more recently, nearly everybody.

ALLIES: Were the first alien species to make contact with Earth. They allowed humans to use their jumpgate technology and travel into hyperspace – thereby enabling them to explore the stars.

ALIEN ARTEFACT: The Eye is an ancient and sacred Centauri artefact, missing for over 100 years. Once the property of the very first Centauri Emperor, it was returned to Londo Mollari by Morden.

* *

DARKANGEL

WHAT IS HE? Vampire-like being that inhabits the transformed moon of Earth, centuries in the future. Described as a "storm of darkness", the feared 'vampyre' plucks Aeriel's friend Eoduin from the mountainside, leading Aeriel to quest for revenge.

MOST LIKELY TO BE DESCRIBED AS: "He is monstrous and evil, but his soul is still his own – there is that final spark of good in him."

* *

DARK-CLOAKED ALIEN

CATEGORY: UFO report.

DATE: 12 September 1952.

LOCATION: West Virginia, USA.

WITNESSES: Kathleen May, Eugene Lemon, Neil Lumley and four other people.

>>>

DARK-CLOAKED ALIEN

APPEARANCE: Sinister humanoid in dark cloak standing 3 metres tall. The being had a red face, with orange beams coming from its eyes.

MISSION: Peaceful exploration.

PLANET OF ORIGIN: Unknown.The being did not attempt to communicate.

ENCOUNTERED WHEN? Hundreds of people across West Virginia saw a bright UFO moving through the sky. The sphere finally landed at Flatwoods and seven local people set out to find it. Approaching up a hill, they began to notice a strange and unpleasant smell in the air. Lemon's dog appeared suddenly terrified and a bank of foul-smelling fog engulfed the group.
At the top of the hill, the group saw a ball of light "the size of a house" and the alien entity itself. The entity floated back into its ship which then took off. Some of the party had to be treated for shock, while others "vomited for hours" as a result of the weird-smelling fog.

AFTER-EFFECTS: The local press and police found landing marks and a strange, oily substance covering the nearby plants. Many of the seven witness suffered painful eyes and sore throats for days afterwards.

* *

EIGHT-FINGERED ALIENS

CATEGORY: UFO report.

DATE: 14 August 1947.

LOCATION: Friuli, Italy.

WITNESSES: Professor Rapuzzi Johannis.

APPEARANCE: Humanoids, one metre tall with large heads and green skin. Their eyes were large, yellow-green and with a vertical pupil. >>>

They were wearing skullcaps and dark blue overalls. Each of their hands had eight fingers, arranged in opposing rows of fours.

MISSION: Peaceful exploration.

ENCOUNTERED WHEN? Professor Johannis was collecting rocks for his geology work in a deserted part of northern Italy when he chanced upon a strange red-coloured craft. There were two small 'children' near the craft, who, the Professor quickly realised, were certainly not human.

He approached nearer, but unfortunately one of the beings interpreted the raising of his arm as an act of aggression and stunned the Professor. He found himself paralysed on the ground and could only watch helplessly as the aliens entered their craft and flew away.

AFTER-EFFECTS: The Professor made a quick and full recovery.

* *

FERENGI

APPEARANCE: Humanoids with orange skin, bald heads and very, very large ears.

WHO ARE THEY? Race of merchants and dealers interested only in making a profit.

PLANET OF ORIGIN: Ferenginar, known for its very wet climate. The Ferengi language has 178 words for "rain".

LIFESTYLE: An extremely sexiest society, with the females prohibited by law from going into business. They are guided by their religious book, the *Rules of Acquisition*, and their leader is the Grand Nagus.

FAMOUS FACE: Quark, owner of Deep Space Nine's bar and casino.

F > G   DATA 7 >>>

FIRE BALLOONS

APPEARANCE: Beautiful spheres of blue light.

WHAT ARE THEY? An ancient species which featured briefly in the *Martian Chronicles*. Fire Balloons are the descendants of an ancient race so old that they have given up physical forms completely, preferring to exist as balls of blue light energy. Only found in isolated mountain areas. They are known to communicate telepathically.

MOST LIKELY TO SAY: "We are the old ones. We are the old Martians, who left our marble cities and went into the hills, forsaking the material life we had once lived. So very long ago that we became these things that we are now."

* *

FRANK-N-FURTER

WHO IS HE? A colourful but misguided amateur scientist from the galaxy of Transylvania.

WHAT HAPPENED? He tried to create the perfect man in the lab of his castle hideaway.

* *

GAMORREAN GUARDS

WHAT ARE THEY? Green, pig-like beings, strong, but slow-witted. Gamorreans are cosmic mercenaries.

WHAT HAPPENED? They were used as palace guards by Jabba the Hutt, but were easily overcome by Luke Skywalker's Jedi mind trick.

GIANTS

WHO ARE THEY? Aliens on a planet where society and biology are mu~~ch~~ like the Earth's, but everything is twelve times the size.

WHAT HAPPENED? When the spaceship *Spindrift* encountered a strange, white cloud during a routine flight, it was transported to an alien planet where the crew and passengers found themselves trapped in the Land of the Giants.

The Giants were attempting to learn more about Earth and had created the white cloud that transported them across space. The Giants were aware of the little travellers and made many attempts to capture them.

WARNING: Earth travellers are strongly advised to avoid the planet of th~~e~~ Giants at all costs.

* *

GLOWING SPECTRE

CATEGORY: UFO report.

DATE: 12 November 1976.

LOCATION: Badajoz, Spain.

WITNESSES: Three members of the Spanish Air Force.

APPEARANCE: Alien apparition nearly three metres tall. The figure was floating in mid-air and emanated a green glow. The humanoid entity was wearing a helmet-like device, although his limbs seemed not to be fully materialised. His hovering image was apparently made out of small points of light – perhaps a projection from a craft somewhere else.

>>~~>~~

GLOWING SPECTRE

PLANET OF ORIGIN: Unknown – the figure vanished without saying a word.

MISSION: Exploration and possible attempt at contact.

ENCOUNTERED WHEN? Three soldiers were on night duty at a Spanish airbase. They were alerted by a shrill, whistling noise and spotted a bright light moving across the sky. Their guard dog began to behave strangely and without further warning the soldiers saw the figure described above appear in front of them. Two of the soldiers fired their weapons at the figure, and after a flash of light it vanished.

AFTER-EFFECTS: None.

* *

JAWAS

APPEARANCE: Small, rodent-like scavengers. They usually wear brown cloaks and their eyes appear as glowing yellow orbs beneath their hoods.

WHO ARE THEY? A scavenger species who travel the harsh deserts of Tatooine, making their living by finding, repairing and then reselling hardware such as droids and transports. They are the dodgy, second-hand car dealers of the galactic community.

PLANET OF ORIGIN: Tatooine – but Jawas are also found on other worlds.

TRANSPORT: Colonies of Jawas travel across the desert wastes in massive, slow-moving transports called sandcrawlers.

WEAPONS: Most carry blasters and various tools that can be used to render droids harmless so they can be 'recovered' easily.

* *

KAZON

WHO ARE THEY? A deeply boring race, split up into many different tribes, always at war with each other. In short, a bunch of galactic losers.

WHAT HAPPENED? They caused trouble for the crew of the *Voyager* after the ship was catapulted 70,000 light years across space into an unknown sector of the galaxy.

* *

LIZARD MEN

CATEGORY: UFO report.

DATE: July 1983.

LOCATION: Missouri, USA.

WITNESSES: Ron and Paula Watson.

APPEARANCE: Green-skinned humanoids with webbed hands and feet.

ENCOUNTERED WHEN? Spotting strange flashes coming from the field opposite their farmhouse, Ron and Paula Watson went to investigate and found a whole collection of alien species – probably the most ever seen together in one place on Earth.

>>>

Two silver-suited beings were leaning down over an unconscious black cow. Behind them was a craft of some kind and standing at its side were two even odder aliens.

On one side were the lizard men, and on the other was a large, hairy creature that resembled Big Foot, which had green eyes with yellow slits. The silver-suited aliens transported the unconscious cow inside their ship which then disappeared.

CLASSIFIED DATA: The witnesses were stunned by what they had seen. The case provides one of the few instances where a cattle mutilation has actually been observed.

* *

MULTI-LIMBED ALIEN

CATEGORY: UFO report.

DATE: August 1955.

LOCATION: California, USA.

WITNESSES: Eight children.

APPEARANCE: Humanoid, but with four legs and four arms – doubled from the elbow down. The creature had large, red eyes, a big, gaping mouth and four-diamond shaped marks where its nose should have been.

MISSION: Exploration and possible attempt at abduction.

ENCOUNTERED WHEN? A group of eight children were playing together when they noticed a silver saucer hovering in the sky nearby. Other craft began to appear and disappear around it, giving out musical notes.

One of the craft landed in a field and the red-eyed alien emerged. The alien asked one of the boys to climb a tree so he could be picked up by the craft a short time later. The boy agreed, but was persuaded to return to the ground by his friends just before the silver saucer circled the tree and disappeared.

>>>

AFTER-EFFECTS: The children were left very frightened by the experience which was recorded by Gordon Creighton as 'The Extraordinary Happenings at Casa Blanca' in *Flying Saucer Review*.

* *

NARN

APPEARANCE: Powerful, humanoid reptiles with red eyes.

WHO ARE THEY? A race that have spent most of their energy for the last few hundred years on hating the Centauri. The Narn home world was conquered by the Centauri Republic twice in recent memory and both times the population was reduced to slaves. Their codes of honour and swordplay are similar to those of ancient Japanese society.

PLANET OF ORIGIN: Narn, ruled by the Kha'Ri – a political body made up of seven circles or groups.

FAMOUS FACE: G'Kar, their ambassador on Babylon 5. G'Kar began his stay on Babylon 5 as a bloodthirsty warrior out for revenge, but time and experience have mellowed him considerably. He put his thoughts down on paper in the *Book of G'Kar* and accidentally became a religious icon.

STRENGTHS: Narn are strong-willed survivors.

WEAKNESSES: Pride and bitterness.

ENEMIES: The Centauri people. The Centauri Republic. In fact, Centauri anything.

MOST LIKELY TO SAY: "I confess that I look forward to the day when we have cleansed the universe of the Centauri and carved their bones into little flutes for Narn children." – G'Kar.

G'KAR

NEMISIS THE WARLOCK

WHO IS HE? Self-proclaimed leader of the Cabal, an interplanetary alien alliance. He is regarded by some races as a saviour. Neither wholly good nor evil, Nemisis has often used his alien magic firmly in favour of Khaos and against the forces of Order in the universe.

PLANET OF ORIGIN: Gandarva, in the mysterious Nether Worlds.

* *

Q

WHO IS HE? An obnoxious, intergalactic prankster who regularly irritated Captain Picard of the starship *Enterprise* during his command.

WHAT HAPPENED? Q has fantastic powers and was responsible for the Federation's first ever encounter with the deadly Borg when he transported the *Enterprise* into Borg space.

* *

SALACIOUS CRUMB

WHO WAS HE? Small, annoying, monkey-like creature and member of Jabba the Hutt's court. Best-known for his maniacal laugh. He died with his fat and bloated master.

SANDWORMS OF DUNE

APPEARANCE: Huge, segmented, silver-grey worms. They can grow up to 400 metres long and 100 metres wide. The creatures have more than 1000 carbosilica teeth which they use to burrow through the ground.

PLANET OF ORIGIN: Arrakis, which is also known as Dune because of its unchanging desert environment. Arrakis is the third planet from its star, Canopus.

LIFESTYLE: Sandworms fall victim to no natural predators on their home world and can live for many years unless attacked by another worm or drowned in water.

They are attracted by any steady vibration and will attack whatever is causing it. The local tribespeople, the Fremen, use irregular strides when they walk. The only safe method of walking normally on the planet's surface is to use a 'thumper' – a device designed to distract a worm's attention.

The Fremen know the worms as *shai-hulud* and use devices called maker-hooks to capture, mount and then ride the Sandworms. To ride a Sandworm without being dragged below the surface and killed is seen, quite rightly, as a sign of adulthood.

MINING: Dune is the only source of the spice 'melange', a priceless commodity which is, among other things, essential to space travel. Spice mining is a dangerous and risky business since drilling can attract the unwanted attentions of a Sandworm at any moment.

MOST LIKELY TO BE DESCRIBED AS:
"The worm is the spice. The spice is the worm."

"Bless the Maker and his water… Bless the coming and going of him. May his passage cleanse the world."

SELENITES

APPEARANCE: Ant-like beings about a metre and a half tall, with whip-like tentacles and bulging eyes.

WHO ARE THEY? Inhabitants of the moon who live in a vast, underground colony. They are ruled by the kindly Grand Lunar (whose brain is several metres across) and live in a crime-free, peaceful world.

PLANET OF ORIGIN: Earth's moon.

LIFESTYLE: To feed themselves, Selenites breed and farm mooncalves, fat beasts over 50 metres long which move like massive worms. Selenites wear protective clothing and helmets when herding mooncalves.

ENCOUNTERED WHEN? The Victorian inventor and explorer Cavor and his partner Bedford became the First Men in the Moon. Cavor journeyed to Earth's moon by means of his invention of Cavorite – anti-gravity paint.

* *

SLAB ALIENS

CATEGORY: UFO report.

DATE: 27 January 1977.

LOCATION: Kentucky, USA.

WITNESSES: Lee Parrish, aged 19.

APPEARANCE: Large, robotic slabs.

PLANET OF ORIGIN: Unknown. Entities did not communicate.

ENCOUNTERED WHEN? Lee Parrish was driving home late at night when he spotted a red-coloured craft moving through the sky. At one point, Parrish suddenly realised that he no longer seemed to be in control of his vehicle. When he arrived home, he was puzzled to find that he had a 30-minute period of missing time.

Parrish volunteered to undergo hypnosis to understand more about his experience. He recalled being taken into a large, white, circular room on board the craft.

In the room were three robotic slabs of different sizes. The tallest was seven metres high, black, and had a handless arm coming out of it. The second entity was only two metres tall and white. Parrish somehow sensed that this one was in control. The third and smallest entity was red and also had one arm.

AFTER-EFFECTS: The encounter left Parrish with sore, bloodshot eyes and the odd feeling that one day he would meet the creatures again.

* *

TALOSIANS

WHO ARE THEY? Humanoids with large, domed heads.

PLANET OF ORIGIN: Talos IV, one of 11 planets orbiting a binary star.

STRENGTHS: They can telepathically project illusions to other life forms.

LIFESTYLE: They have collected a menagerie of creatures from other worlds.

HISTORY: Their ancestors were nearly wiped out by a terrible war in their distant past. The Talosians migrated underground and developed their mental powers. For a long period, Federation General Order 7 forbade contact with their planet. The ex-Captain of the *Enterprise*, Christopher Pike, is now their permanent guest.

TRIBBLES

WHAT ARE THEY? Small, round balls of self-replicating trouble. Tribbles eat anything within their reach and can multiply at the rate of several thousand per hour. Tribbles are much hated by all Klingons.

ENCOUNTERED WHEN? They caused problems for Captain Kirk aboard the K-9 space station.

TUSKEN RAIDERS
(AKA SAND PEOPLE)

APPEARANCE: They wear sand-coloured robes, protective goggles and masks.

WHO ARE THEY? Inhabitants of the harsh, desert lands of Tatooine.

LIFESTYLE: They are prone to violence and carry their traditional weapon – the *gaderffii* or *gaffi* stick – with them at all times. They use Banthas, large beasts of burden, to help them survive in the sandy wastes (see page 172).

ENCOUNTERED BY? Unwary travellers often find themselves victims of Sand People attacks. They have also been known to raid small settlements. One group made the mistake of kidnapping Shmi Skywalker, mother of Anakin Skywalker. When the Jedi-trained youth returned to Tatooine he tracked down the raiding party and found his mother, only to have her die in his arms. Skywalker avenged her death by slaughtering the entire camp.

* *

VOGONS

APPEARANCE: Green, rubbery-skinned aliens with pig-like, ugly faces.

PLANET OF ORIGIN: Vogsphere.

NATURE: *The Hitch Hiker's Guide to the Galaxy* describes Vogons as "one of the most unpleasant races in the galaxy" before going on to conclude that "the best way to get a drink out of a Vogon is to stick your fingers down his throat". The worst thing about them, however, is their poetry.

TRADITIONS: Once a year the Vogons import 27,000 jewelled scuttling crabs and spend the night smashing them to bits with large, iron mallets.

VORLONS

APPEARANCE: Vorlons always wear 'encounter suits' when in the presence of other races. No one has actually seen a Vorlon for centuries, although their 'true' form is rumoured to resemble a luminescent jellyfish.

WHO ARE THEY? One of the galaxy's most ancient and powerful races. Locked in an eternal war with the Shadows.

PLANET OF ORIGIN: Shrouded in secrecy. Visitors are not allowed into Vorlon space.

STRENGTHS: Advanced technology that can appear almost godlike in its powers.

WEAKNESSES: Prone to over-interfere in the affairs of the other 'lesser' races. Fear of the Shadows.

FAMOUS FACE: Their representative on Babylon 5 was Ambassador Kosh who formed a close relationship with Captain John Sheridan. Kosh was later killed by the Shadows and replaced by another ambassador.

BATTLE TACTICS: Vorlons have been manipulating the genetics of the younger races for thousands of years. They created telepaths on several worlds so they could be used as weapons against the Shadows next time they emerged.

The Vorlons like to portray themselves as the galactic good guys, but the truth is that they have their own agenda of self-interest and have meddled in the evolution of other races.

Vorlons abducted the serial killer known as Jack the Ripper from Earth in the year 1888 to use as a kind of evil inquisitor.

ALIEN ARTEFACT: Gateway to Thirdspace – an ancient Vorlon

experiment to open a doorway to another dimension, beyond normal space or hyperspace. It was an experiment which went horribly wrong. Found drifting in hyperspace, the Gateway was recovered and later destroyed by the personnel of Babylon 5.

MOST LIKELY TO SAY: Anything mysterious. Vorlon utterances known as Koshisms include:

"Understanding is a three-edged sword."

"A stroke of the brush does not guarantee art from the bristles."

"The avalanche has already started. It is too late for the pebbles to vote."

AMBASSADOR KOSH

WALL-WALKER

CATEGORY: UFO report.

DATE: December 1973.

LOCATION: Vilvoorde, Belgium.

WITNESSES: Name withheld at request of witness.

APPEARANCE: One-metre tall humanoid wearing a shiny, one-piece spacesuit complete with goldfish-bowl helmet. It had pointed ears and large, yellow eyes.

ENCOUNTERED WHEN? The witness went to his kitchen to fix a late-night snack when he noticed a green glow coming from the garden.

Looking out of the window he spotted the being, who was examining the ground with a device similar to a metal detector.

The witness got the being's attention by flashing a torch at it, at which point the little figure moved around in very jerky movements to face him. Seeing it was under observation, the being stuck up two fingers in a V-sign and headed for the garden wall.

The figure left the garden by walking straight up the garden wall and over it. Moments later the witness saw a bright sphere take off and head skyward.

MISSION: Obviously not the most diplomatic of aliens, probably here on a scientific survey.

ALIEN ADVICE: Erm… basically, "Get stuffed!"

WATTO

APPEARANCE: A tubby, blue-skinned Toydarian with wings which allow him to hover.

WHO IS HE? Watto runs a spare parts junk shop on Tatooine. He is a quick-witted merchant with a knack for haggling and cannot be affected by Jedi mind tricks. He loves money and gambling. He has had at least two human slaves – Shmi and Anakin Skywalker. He lost Anakin as the result of a badly misjudged bet.

* *

WOMP RATS

WHAT ARE THEY? Meat-eating rodents that live in the desert canyons of Tatooine. They grow to be three metres long and hunt in packs.

* *

WORMHOLE ALIENS

(AKA THE PROPHETS)

WHO ARE THEY? A race of very powerful entities. They exist outside of time and space in the stable wormhole near Deep Space Nine. They are worshipped as gods by the Bajorans for whom the wormhole is a special, mystic place.

MOST LIKELY TO BE DESCRIBED AS: "The Prophets will Always Walk with Us. The Prophets will Always Guide Us."

ZANTI MISFITS

APPEARANCE: Large bugs with ugly, humanoid faces.

WHO WERE THEY? Criminals from the planet Zanti, exiled to Earth because the rulers of their home world were incapable of carrying out capital punishment on their own kind.

The Zanti Misfits are rumoured to originate somewhere in the Outer Limits of space and were transported to Earth on board *Penal Ship One*. Upon their arrival, they were quarantined by the military in a desert ghost town, but a series of chance incidents resulted in the entire group of Zanti criminals being killed by the soldiers.

AFTER-EFFECTS: The planet Zanti did not retaliate. Apparently, the death of their criminals and misfits at the hands (and feet) of humans was their plan all along.

* *

ZELDA

WHO IS SHE? Witch Queen of the planet Guk. She used Mars as a temporary base to attack the Earth in the year 2020.

WHO DEFENDED EARTH? The Terrahawks, an international taskforce devoted to protecting the planet from Zelda's evil schemes.

DATA 7 COMPLETE

ALIEN KIDNAPPERS

A constant danger for any human is the threat of being spacenapped by a technologically superior race eager to try out the medical probe collection on their new spacecraft. The good news for the galactic tourist is that you have far more chance of being kidnapped from Earth than while on your travels. This data file looks at the cosmic kidnappers you might meet.

(Useful information: Humans who feel they have been treated roughly or unfairly may make a formal complaint to the SCC (Spacenapping Complaints Commission) c/o Zzulk Town Hall, Cardax Prime, Dollex. These must be made in red ink in triplicate and be delivered in person. In extreme cases the aliens involved may have their spacenapping licence suspected or even revoked.)

>>>

THE COLLECTOR

APPEARANCE: Usually appears in the form of a frail, elderly man, although it is thought that his true form is far more powerful and considerably more alien in nature.

WHO IS HE? Member of the Elders. The Collector is incredibly old and has been hanging about since just after the Big Bang.

LIFESTYLE: He is dedicated to obtaining an example of every life form in the galaxy. Has had several confrontations with the Earth-based superhero group the Avengers and has kidnapped various members on many occasions.

WHAT DID HE WANT? The Collector's most evil masterplan was his intended use of the alien race 'the Brethren' as an unwitting biological weapon with which he planned to devastate the Earth. He then intended to capture the few survivors of humanity for his collection (thereby ensuring their uniqueness and value).

The Collector also has powers of prophecy, allowing him to see certain future events and potential disasters. However, it should be noted that this time-spanning power has hardly ever helped him avoid defeat in his evil schemes. The Collector appeared to die at one point, but was later brought back to life by the Grandmaster (a fellow Elder) who lost his own life as a result.

WEAPONS: Temporal assimilator (i.e. a time-travel device), a cloak of levitation and advanced teleportation technology. He can also manipulate cosmic energy for a variety of uses, such as attacking foes and creating forcefields.

MOST LIKELY TO SAY: "There is no dishonour in accepting the inevitable! Submit! It would be a shame if I accidentally damaged you beyond repair while subduing you!"

GIANT BRAINS

CATEGORY: UFO report.

DATE: 17 August 1971.

LOCATION: Dapple Gray Lane, South Los Angeles, California, USA.

WITNESSES: John Hodges and Pete Rodriguez.

APPEARANCE: Two giant, wrinkled brains.

PLANET OF ORIGIN: Claimed to be from Zeta Reticuli (quite a popular choice for visiting aliens).

ENCOUNTERED WHEN? Hodges and Rodriguez were returning to their car at 2.00 am when they saw two strange beings in front of it, which they later described as disembodied brains. The men stared at the odd creatures for a few minutes then drove away.

When they returned home they realised that they had two hours of missing time to account for. Years later under hypnosis, Hodges claimed he was taken on board a craft of some kind where tall, grey beings were present – possibly the brains' real masters.

ALIEN ADVICE: One of the tall beings told Hodges that the brain was merely a translator. The aliens were carefully observing Earth because of the danger of humankind destroying the planet with atomic weapons. Hodges was shown a vision of a dead, barren Earth. The creatures also claimed that human beings are the result of alien DNA experiments conducted over millions of years.

AFTER-EFFECTS: Hodges had a further encounter with the creatures in 1978. However, after several of the predictions they gave him turned out to be wildly inaccurate, Hodges decided that, although real, the beings simply could not be trusted.

GREY CLAWED ALIENS

CATEGORY: UFO report.

DATE: 11 October 1973.

LOCATION: Mississippi, USA.

WITNESSES: Shipyard workers Charlie Hickson and Calvin Parker.

APPEARANCE: One and a half metres tall with thick, grey skin covered in wrinkles, rather like an elephant's. Their long arms ended in pincer-like claws.

MISSION: Abduction for medical experiments.

ENCOUNTERED WHEN? The two witnesses were night fishing from a wooden pier on the Pascagoula River. They noticed a bright-blue light in the sky coming towards them. The oval-shaped craft floated just above the water and one end opened, revealing three alien beings. They floated though the air towards the terrified men, picked both of them up and returned to the ship with them.

The men spent about 20 minutes inside before being replaced on the pier, somewhat dazed.

MOST LIKELY TO SAY: "I was scared to death... so scared you can't imagine." – Charlie Hickson.

ALIEN ADVICE: None offered, as far as the witnesses could remember. This sighting was one of a whole wave over America in October 1973.

AFTER-EFFECTS: Knowing they would not be believed, but unable to remain silent, the men reported their experience to a local airbase and the nearby sheriff. Hickson and his family have had several other strange events happen to them since, but have always refused to sell their stories for money.

GULF BREEZE ALIENS

CATEGORY: UFO report.

DATE: November 1987.

LOCATION: Florida, USA.

WITNESSES: Ed Walters.

APPEARANCE: Small humanoids with large, dark eyes. They wore protective helmets of some kind.

ENCOUNTERED WHEN? Walters began seeing UFOs in November 1987, and a month later had his first contact with their occupants. Late one night, Walters got out of bed to look around the house for intruders. Opening the curtains to his French doors, he was confronted by a small alien being. The creature backed away as the doors opened and Walters believes that a flash of blue light beamed the entity back to its hovering spaceship.

MISSION: Investigation and contact.

AFTER-EFFECTS: The Gulf Breeze case became one of America's most famous. Walters claimed to have had many abduction experiences and to have taken rolls of film of the UFOs. Some of the events were witnessed by other people.

* *

GUN-HAND ALIENS

CATEGORY: UFO report.

DATE: 25 October 1974.

LOCATION: Wyoming, USA.

WITNESSES: Carl Higdon.

APPEARANCE: Humanoid with no chin or jaw and two antennae on his forehead. The 2-metre tall being had yellow skin, small eyes and no visible ears.

PLANET OF ORIGIN: Described as a dark planet 163,000 light years away.

ENCOUNTERED WHEN? Higdon was in the woods on a hunting expedition. When he aimed his gun at an elk and fired, he saw the bullet leave his gun very slowly and fall gently to the ground. He realised that the area of woodland around him was utterly silent and saw a man approaching from across the clearing. As he drew nearer, Higdon saw that the being was not human – he had no hands and his right arm ended in a cone-shaped, gun device.

The figure asked Higdon, "How you doin'?" and introduced himself as Ausso. This is one of the few occasions when a visiting alien has told a human his name. Higdon was taken into the being's cube-shaped craft where he saw five elks frozen in a chamber.

WHAT HAPPENED NEXT? Ausso operated the ship's controls and Higdon saw them move away from the Earth. Only moments later they landed on Ausso's planet. Higdon was fascinated to see other, apparently normal, humans on the planet. They did not appear to be prisoners or held against their will.

One of the structures on the aliens' planet was a space-needle-type building surrounded by very bright spotlights. Higdon shielded his eyes, complaining they were too bright. The alien replied, "Your sun burns us."

Higdon was given a medical examination and then told that he had failed – he was not what they were looking for. He was transported back to the woodlands of Wyoming and left near his truck.

>>>

MISSION: Exploration and the capture of five elk. Higdon's experience also suggests that the aliens were looking for humans to live permanently on their home world. Similar aliens were sighted in Wales two years later – perhaps indicating regular visits to Earth.

AFTER-EFFECTS: Higdon found the single bullet that he had fired and seen fall to the ground. It was examined and found to be in a strange condition. Several other witnesses not connected to Higdon reported seeing lights in the sky over the woodlands that night.

* *

THE HIVE

WHO ARE THEY? Aliens intent on taking over Earth by infiltrating the US government and its secret services. The Hive were the real cause of the Kennedy assassination in 1963 and have been dictating much of America's history since the Roswell saucer crash of 1947.

APPEARANCE: Spider-legged, slug-like parasites that enter their hosts by the mouth.

MISSION: Total domination of the human species.

* *

KANAMIT

WHO ARE THEY? Arrived on Earth in huge flying saucers seemingly on a diplomatic mission of peace. They extended an invitation for humans to visit their world somewhere in the Twilight Zone of space. The real purpose of their visit was revealed when a human decoding expert learned that their book *To Serve Man* was actually a cookery book.

METALUNANS

WHO ARE THEY? Alien species involved in a war with the planet Zahgon, who have been attacking their planet's energy shield.

PLANET OF ORIGIN: The rocky, barren world of Metaluna. The natives live in underground dwellings.

WHAT HAPPENED? They abducted top Earth scientists Cal Meachum and Ruth Adams.

WHY? To add their brain power to the efforts to save Metaluna. Passing an intelligence test, Meachum finds himself taken from "this Island Earth" to Metaluna. Arriving too late to save the protective barrier, the humans were attacked by an injured mutant slave before being helped to return to Earth.

* *

SOUTH PARK ALIENS

WHO ARE THEY? They look like a variation on the traditional Grey, but even more sinister.

WHAT HAPPENED? They kidnapped the unsuspecting Cartman and subjected him to terrible medical experiments.

The aliens also spacenapped Kyle's little brother Eric, causing Cartman even more distress.

WHAT HAPPENED NEXT? They killed Kenny.

SNACK MOST LIKELY TO HELP YOU GET OVER AN ALIEN ABDUCTION: Cheezy Poofs.

LEAST LIKELY TO SAY: "Sweet!"

* *

TECHNOBOTS

APPEARANCE: Silver autobots.

WHO ARE THEY? Self-replicating robots who scavenge the universe for abandoned items of useful technology. Their favourite finds are drifting space wrecks and long-lost civilisations.

CURRENT HOME WORLD: Their planet Technobabble is located beyond the Trifid Nebula. Its capital city, Techno Central, is an impressive expanse of silver spires and gleaming metal walkways.

LIFESTYLE: Basically lazy, unless annoyed. Technobots live in family units who look after and help repair each other. They are not above stealing items which have particularly taken their fancy.

Their planet is controlled by the Great Thinking Machine, which takes care of their daily needs such as food, power charges and turning all the lights out when it's time for bed.

PLANET OF ORIGIN: Even the Technobots are unsure of their exact point of origin. Records in the Inter-Galactic Robot-Patent Office suggest that their original design was the creation of the notorious genius

>>>

Professor J Cummins, a well-known inventor and professional astro-bankrupt from the planet Warez.

STRENGTHS: Their technology is cobbled together from the items and devices they have salvaged and stolen from other races.

Their rocket science is very advanced and uses hyper-warp outside inhabited solar systems (and, when no one's looking, sometimes inside). They can also open inter-dimensional gateways for short periods.

WEAKNESSES: Although always handy with a sonic screwdriver, they are not known for being the brightest brains in the universe. When the Great Thinking Machine went wrong, it plunged their entire planet into darkness and despair. They resorted to kidnapping the human known as Cosmic Kev in the hope that he would repair it for them. He succeeded, but then escaped, beginning a long chase that resulted in a shoot-out and the near-destruction of the Imperial Museum of Art on Zinbarr.

WEAPONS: Blaster guns of various designs, depending on where they've stolen them.

BATTLE TACTICS: They will only fight if the odds are greatly in their favour. Otherwise, they prefer discretion as the better part of valour.

MOST LIKELY TO SAY: "No worry. We throwing you into space. Find someone else fixy."

* *

THREE-EYED ALIENS

CATEGORY: UFO report.

DATE: 6 December 1978.

LOCATION: Genoa, Italy.

WITNESSES: Fortunato Zanfretta.

APPEARANCE: The beings were three metres tall, covered with thick, green hair and had two pointed ears on the side of their heads. Each had two large, yellow eyes, with a third smaller eye positioned centrally just above.

MISSION: Abduction for medical experiments.

THREE-EYED ALIENS

ENCOUNTERED WHEN? Nightwatchman Zanfretta saw four strange lights moving oddly in a nearby garden. He attempted to call for help but found that his radio would not work. Under hypnotic regression weeks later, he remembered meeting tall, green aliens who forced him on to their ship and into a hot, round room. There they performed a painful experiment on his head before releasing him.

* *

TUJUNGA CANYON ALIENS

CATEGORY: UFO report.

DATE: 22 March 1953.

LOCATION: Tujunga Canyon, California, USA.

WITNESSES: Sara Shaw and Jan Whitley.

APPEARANCE: Very thin, all-black humanoids. Eyes were their only facial feature.

ENCOUNTERED WHEN? The two women were woken at 2.00 am by a bright light shining in the windows of the isolated house. The next moment they checked the time and were amazed to find that two hours had passed seemingly in the blink of an eye. Disturbed by the incident, they felt that something else had occurred. Later, under hypnotic regression, they both recalled being taken on board a saucer-shaped ship and undergoing a medical examination.

MISSION: Abduction and medical examination of humans.

ALIEN ADVICE: Only that the abductees would forget all that had happened to them.

TURTLE-HEADED ALIENS

CATEGORY: UFO report.

DATE: 26 August 1972.

LOCATION: Northern Maine, USA.

WITNESSES: Charlie Fotz, Chuck Rak, Jim and Jack Weiner.

APPEARANCE: Just under two metres tall, the most distinctive feature was their turtle-like head. They had large eyes but no nose. Each hand had four fingers and they wore one-piece jumpsuits.

ENCOUNTERED WHEN? The four witnesses were on a canoeing expedition and were attempting some night fishing. They spotted a very bright sphere of light which descended towards them, shining a blue beam.

The rest of the experience was recalled later under hypnosis. The four friends had been taken on board the craft and given medical examinations. The aliens spoke to the men telepathically before returning them to their boat unharmed.

MISSION: Scientific examination of humans.

AFTER-EFFECTS: As in many similar cases, all four men experienced interrupted sleep patterns afterwards.

DATA 8 COMPLETE

- >

ALIEN MONSTERS AND CREATURES

It is an unfortunate fact of cosmic life that humans are a rather puny and weak species, and therefore prone at some stage in their travels to become a light snack for another life form.

When encountering any of the species in Data File 9, you are sincerely advised to adopt the 'leg defence'. In this complex manoeuvre, you should put one leg in front of the other very, very, very quickly and move in the opposite direction from whatever is calculating your calorific value.

>>>

ALIENS

APPEARANCE: The fully grown adult stands nearly three metres tall, with a tough, black exoskeleton. It has a large, curved head with enormous jaws, and a second set of jaws inside its mouth. Its blood is organic acid, capable of eating through most metals.

WHAT ARE THEY? The deadliest creatures in the universe.

PLANET OF ORIGIN: Their original home planet remains unknown. Humankind first encountered this species, known only as 'Aliens', when the spaceship *Nostromo* landed on Acheron. The only survivors of that incident were Warrant Officer Ripley and the ship's cat, Jones.

LIFE CYCLE: The Alien's breeding cycle uses other life forms as the host for its young. An Alien 'face-hugger' attaches itself to the victim's face and inserts a tube down the throat to deposit an egg or seed inside the victim's body. The baby Alien grows there and after some days bursts out of its now redundant host, killing it in the process. An Alien queen stands five metres tall and can produce hundreds of eggs at a time.

WEAKNESSES: None.

WEAPONS: Claws, teeth, acid blood.

ENEMIES: Anything that moves.

CLASSIFIED DATA: The crew of the *Nostromo* were deliberately exposed to the Alien by their employers 'the Company', who wanted one of the creatures brought back to Earth as a potential biological weapon.

Many years later, Ripley returned to Acheron in the company of US Colonial Marines, only to find the human colony there overrun with Aliens. The Alien creatures have also been reported on the prison planet of Fiorina 161, killing several of the inmates. >>

ALIEN MONSTERS & CREATURES

Centuries later, the Company tried to replicate an Alien queen by using fragmented DNA remains from the prison planet. After several failed attempts, this programme led eventually to the creation of near-perfect clones of both Ripley and an Alien.

* *

BUGS

WHAT ARE THEY? Deadly, insectoid killers.

PLANET OF ORIGIN: Klendathu, an orange world ringed by an asteroid belt. It orbits a double star.

THE BUG WAR:
The Bugs launched an asteroid that destroyed an entire Earth city. Humans then took the war to the enemy.

TYPES OF BUGS: Bugs come in all shapes and sizes, each one more deadly than the last.

Warrior Bugs – the most common and aggressive bugs. They are used as foot soldiers during combat.
Hopper Bugs – very fast; can remove a man's head without breaking stride.
Tanker Bugs – huge bugs that can fire a corrosive chemical which eats through anything it touches.
Brain Bugs – the secret intelligence behind the Bug army. One was captured by humans towards the end of the first great campaign.

ENEMIES: All humankind, especially Starship Troopers.

WARNING: Galactic travellers are advised to avoid contact with all species of Bugs.

* *

CHUPACABRA

APPEARANCE: Most often described as a half man, half beast, with vampire fangs and a long, snake-like tongue. It has a row of spikes or quills running down its spine and could possibly be some kind of reptile-hybrid.

LIFESTYLE: Drains blood from animals. Many witnesses in Puerto Rico have seen the creature and sometimes interrupted its feeding. The name Chupacabra means 'goat-sucker', although its victims have also included dogs, cats, horses and cattle.

WHAT IS IT? Latest theories suggest that the Chupacabra may have been left behind – either deliberately or accidentally – by a visiting alien. There have been sightings in other locations around the world, suggesting that the creatures are growing in number.

PLANET OF ORIGIN: Unknown.

STRENGTHS: Fast and intelligent. Some witnesses suggest that it has a limited, chameleon-like ability that enables it to change colour and blend in with its background.

MISSION: Unknown, but reports indicate a strong link between UFOs and the Chupacabras. Luminous, white discs have been reported over the locations where the dreaded 'goat-sucker' has been seen shortly afterwards.

CTHULHU

APPEARANCE: Described by one witness as: "A pulpy, tentacled head on a grotesque and scaly body with long, narrow wings. It was a monster of vaguely anthropoid outline, but with an octopus-like head whose face was a mass of feelers, a scaly, rubbery-looking body, with huge claws on hind and forefeet."

WHAT IS IT? A timeless and immensely powerful being from the nether world of the cosmos. Cthulhu is the leader of the Old Ones. (See also page 157.)

HISTORY: Cthulhu dates from before the dawn of man and is one of a race of monstrous beings whose intelligence and physical form are so strange that they can hardly be comprehended by the human mind. Most life forms which have encountered any of the great Old Ones over the years have been driven insane as a result.

LIFESTYLE: The Old Ones wait in a deathless sleep, hidden from the eyes of lesser beings. Some say they hide deep in the oceans of Earth, others that they lie in wait beyond the galactic rim, or even that they lurk in another dimension.

Cthulhu and the Old Ones are waiting "for the stars to be right" before they can return and claim what is rightfully theirs – including the planet Earth.

ALIEN ARTEFACT: A legendary book – the *Necronomicon* – is rumoured to include rites of worship for these monstrous, alien, elder gods, as well as containing stories and secret knowledge from the ancient, darker times. It was written by Abdul Alhazred. The original Arabic title was *Al Azif*, a reference to the night-time sound insects make that was once believed to be the noise of demons howling.

>>>

Like many people involved with Cthulhu, the author came to a sticky end when he was set upon by an invisible monster that devoured him alive in a public street in broad daylight. One of the few known copies of this work was housed in the Miskatonic University Library in Arkham, USA. Understandably, it is kept under constant guard.

FAMOUS FACE: The best-known human associated with the great Cthulhu was the writer H P Lovecraft. His stories about Cthulhu were published as fiction, but when he revealed that his source of inspiration was in fact a series of very vivid dreams, researchers began to realise that his dreams could really be messages from the Old Ones themselves.

* *

CYCLOPEANS

WHAT ARE THEY? Giant, Martian rock snakes. These highly dangerous and hostile creatures spit powerful, destructive blasts from their mouths.

WHAT HAPPENED? After Cyclopeans attacked and damaged a mission to Mars, International Rescue's Thunderbirds team had to help the craft return safely to Earth.

* *

DARK SOLDIERS

WHAT ARE THEY? Invisible servants of the Shadows, said to be five metres tall and horned.

LIFESTYLE: Feed on the internal organs of their victims. One got loose on Babylon 5 but was tracked down by Security Chief Michael Garibaldi.

GORN

WHO ARE THEY? Intelligent, humanoid reptiles. Captain Kirk was forced to battle one on the planet Cestus III with the survival of the *Enterprise* at stake.

* *

'HOLE IN SPACE' ALIENS

CATEGORY: UFO report.

DATE: 8 August 1993.

LOCATION: Victoria, Australia.

WITNESSES: Kelly and Bill Cahill.

APPEARANCE: Over two metres tall and totally black in colour – as if they were "a hole in space". The creatures had long arms, a repulsive pot belly and alarming red eyes.

MISSION: Something very sinister.

ENCOUNTERED WHEN? Heading home after midnight, the Cahills turned a corner in the winding road through the Dandenong foothills and found themselves confronted by a craft hanging silently over the road in front of them.

The ship was about 50 metres wide and while they were watching it, Kelly noticed the black alien standing nearby on the ground. Kelly began to worry as she saw the creature being joined by many others out of the darkness. She had a very strong feeling that the aliens were evil, soulless creatures.

>>>

ALIEN ADVICE: None given.

AFTER-EFFECTS: Kelly suffered from a series of nightmares and had great trouble sleeping. It soon emerged that the entire encounter had been witnessed by another couple whose car was travelling along the road behind the Cahills'.

The case was reported by Bill Chalker as 'An Extraordinary Encounter in the Dandenong Foothills' in *International UFO Reporter*.

* *

HORTA

WHAT ARE THEY? Silicon-based, egg-laying life form. Every 50,000 years, the entire race of Horta die except for one mother who remains alive to guard its eggs and begin the next generation of the species. Horta eggs look like gold spheres about the size of a football.

PLANET OF ORIGIN: Janus VI.

WHAT HAPPENED? A Horta's eggs were damaged by workers on the pergium mining colony. A Vulcan mind-meld from Mr Spock revealed the Horta to be an intelligent and peaceful creature.

JELLYFISH

CATEGORY: UFO report.

DATE: 29 December 1990.

LOCATION: Saga Prefecture, Japan.

WITNESSES: Local cattle farmer.

APPEARANCE: White jellyfish able to float above the ground.

ENCOUNTERED WHEN? Woken by the sound of his dog barking madly, the farmer rushed from his bed to investigate.

His mind went back to a similar incident almost exactly two years before when he had also heard loud and constant barking from the farm dog. On that first occasion the farmer had ignored it and the next day he had found the mutilated body of one of his cows.

This time the farmer raced out to the cowshed right away. There he was startled by the sight of a multi-tentacled jellyfish floating in the air above the body of an injured cow. The jellyfish floated slowly out of the cowshed and then disappeared – leaving the farmer rubbing his eyes in stunned disbelief.

* *

KRELL'S ID MONSTERS

APPEARANCE: Invisible.

WHO ARE THEY? The Krell were a vastly ancient and powerful race who once resided on Altair-4 (aka the Forbidden Planet) and suddenly vanished overnight.

JELLYFISH

ENCOUNTERED BY: The remains of their once great civilisation were discovered by Earth scientist Edward Morbius, who made his home on Altair-4 with his daughter Altaira and Robby the Robot.

The Krell (occasionally shown in records as 'Krel') left behind them a huge, underground, scientific research complex, which Morbius had been exploring during his time on the planet. The Krell's last and greatest scientific achievement was to perfect the ability to create and project matter by the power of thought alone.

Unlike Morbius, the crew of the visiting spacecraft, *Cruiser C-57D*, realised that it was this new power that must have destroyed the Krell. Although as a race they had near-total control over the sciences, they had not learned the same discipline over their subconscious minds. Accidentally, they created terrible monsters that killed every last Krell.

WHAT HAPPENED? When *Cruiser C-57D* was attacked by an invisible id-monster set lose by Morbius's hostile feelings towards the crew, the truth becomes obvious to everyone. Morbius, appalled at his own creation, ensured the planet's destruction while the crew and his daughter fled to safety.

* *

MAN-EATER OF SURREY GREEN

WHAT IS IT? Intelligent plant creature that can exert telepathic influence over people. The species drifts through space waiting to find a world rich in protein where it can feed.

WHAT HAPPENED? One was brought to Earth attached to a returning spacecraft in the 1960s, and ended up in Surrey, England. It was destroyed with acid plant killer by John Steed and Mrs Emma Peel (aka the Avengers).

MOTHMAN

CATEGORY: UFO report as described in John Keel's report *The Mothman Prophecies*.

APPEARANCE: Large, dark figure with huge, bat-like wings. Sometimes described as having glowing red eyes, other times as having no head at all. Either webbed or clawed feet.

MISSION: Seemingly to scare the living daylights out of people.

ENCOUNTERED WHEN? Mothman has been seen at various locations around the world. In a wave of sightings in West Virginia, USA, in November and December 1966, many witnesses reported seeing a dark, bird-like entity with glowing red eyes. The creature was two metres long with a wingspan of over three metres.

An English sighting of a similar creature occurred on 16 November 1963 in Kent, when John Flaxton, Mervyn Hutchingson and their girlfriends watched as a "very bright star" came hurtling out of the sky towards them. A glowing light appeared near them, and minutes later a tall, sinister figure stumbled out of the trees towards them.

* *

MYNOCKS

APPEARANCE: Space bats.

WHAT ARE THEY? Flying parasites that resemble bats. Mynocks can grow to have a wingspan of up to one and a half metres.

LIFESTYLE: They feed from the power cables of passing spacecraft.

* *

NABOO SWAMP CREATURES

WHAT ARE THEY? Varied selection of alien wildlife including:

The **Nuna** , a long-necked, flightless bird that feeds on plants and frogs. The beautiful blue **Peko Peko** bird, which is nearly three metres long from head to tail and has a very powerful jaw.

* *

PITCH-BLACK ALIENS

WHAT ARE THEY? Vicious, flesh-eating aliens encountered by a group of marooned space travellers on a seemingly lifeless world. The pitch-black aliens cannot stand light and emerge only in the dark.

PRAYING MANTIS

CATEGORY: UFO report.

DATE: 1973.

LOCATION: Maryland, USA.

WITNESSES: Mike Shea – a law student at the University of Baltimore.

APPEARANCE: Black insects 2 metres tall. They resembled huge grasshoppers and seemed to be wearing some kind of dark armour. Three of the aliens were very tall, while the fourth was much shorter and seemed to be older than his companions.

PLANET OF ORIGIN: Unknown.

ENCOUNTERED WHEN? Mike Shea was driving to meet a friend one evening when he suddenly saw a beam of intense white light cutting through the night. The source of the light was a huge, saucer-like craft hovering over the road. The ship had a ring of red and yellow lights around it and, despite its size, made absolutely no sound.

As he drove past, Shea just had time to see a group of four insect aliens at the roadside. Then a light blinded him and he found himself on board the ship. He was put on to an examination table; the aliens took skin and hair samples before returning him to his car.

MISSION: Medical research.

AFTER-EFFECTS: Shea had no conscious memory of his encounter, only an awareness of a period of missing time and a feeling of unease. It was over a decade later when Mike finally recalled the alien encounter during hypnotic sessions with researcher Budd Hopkins.

RANCOR

APPEARANCE: Huge, bipedal creatures with an enormous mouth full of teeth.

ENCOUNTERED BY: One was given to Jabba the Hutt as a birthday gift. He kept it to eat his enemies until it was killed by Luke Skywalker.

WHAT HAPPENED? Luke utilised his Jedi talents during the fight and the great brute met its demise when it was impaled under its own gate. Its death was mourned only by its human keeper.

* *

REGILLIAN SEWER RATS

WHAT ARE THEY? Small, unpleasant creatures with teeth at both ends. Encountered by Cosmic Kev during his escape from the Technobots.

* *

REPTOIDS

APPEARANCE: Reptilian aliens with green skin that stand more than two metres tall.

PLANET OF ORIGIN: Rumoured to be a distant world in space (or an alternative universe) where dinosaurs evolved but did not become extinct, instead evolving further into a form of intelligent humanoid.

LIFESTYLE: Often abduct humans. Victims sense a sinister purpose behind this species' actions. Reptoids have been seen with Greys, and reportedly sometimes use hypnosis to appear as Greys to humans.

REPTOIDS

SAND SHARKS OF MARS

WHAT ARE THEY? Dinosaur-like creatures that swam in the sands on the red planet. They menaced the crew of the M-2 Mars probe from Earth in the Outer Limits project.

* *

SARLACC

WHAT IS IT? Flesh-eating creature from the Tatooine desert that swallowed its victims whole. Only the repulsive creature's huge, gaping mouth and tentacles are visible above the sandline of the Great Pit of Carkoon. The creature was used by Jabba the Hutt to get rid of prisoners he especially disliked.

LIFESTYLE: According to local legend, the stomach pit of the Sarlacc has adapted to keep its prey alive for a thousand years, dissolving its victims slowly and painfully.

* *

SPACE SLUGS

WHAT ARE THEY? Fantastically large, worm-like creatures that can survive in the vacuum of space. They live within asteroids. Han Solo accidentally flew the *Millennium Falcon* into one during his flight from the Empire's attack on Hoth.

Space slugs can grow to be as big as 900 metres – longer even than the Sandworms of Dune. Like the Horta, they are silicon-based life forms who can feed on the mineral content of rock.

SPACE SLUG

* *

SPECIES 8472

WHAT ARE THEY? Aliens from another universe, one based on fluid rather than a vacuum. They were encountered by the Borg, who tried and failed to assimilate them. The aliens then began to launch destructive raids into our universe, in the belief that all other intelligent life forms should be destroyed. Species 8472 have five different sexes and their advanced technology is biogenetically engineered.

WARNING: Very dangerous and should be avoided at all costs.

WAMPA ICE CREATURES

WHAT ARE THEY? Native to the snowy wastes of the planet Hoth. One of the white-furred creatures nearly made a meal out of Luke Skywalker and lost an arm as a result.

* *

YMIR

WHAT WAS IT? Brought back "20 million miles to Earth" as an egg, the giant Ymir soon hatched and grew into a huge, green, reptile creature. A power cut set the confused Venusian creature free and it went on a rampage in Rome.

DATA 9 COMPLETE

GAT

DATA 1

DATA 2

DATA 3

DATA 4

DATA 5

DATA 6

DATA 7

DATA 8

DATA 9

DATA 10

So you think you're ready to explore the galaxy?

Can't wait to wander round a lost Martian city? Want to jump through the Guardian of Forever? Planning a picnic on the sands of Dune? Want to hole up in the Bug nests of Klendathu on a wet Thursday afternoon?

It might come as something of a shock to learn that the World Government doesn't hand out a galactic passport to just anyone. Before you can even leave the atmosphere, you need to prove that you won't be a social embarrassment to your home world and to show that you won't bring shame and humiliation on your species by saying the wrong thing at a cosmic cocktail party.

>>>

The GAT (Galactic Aptitude Test) is a recognised interstellar exam which has been written by some of the biggest brains (and longest tentacles) in the universe.

Score 180 or more and the galaxy awaits.

Answers at the end, but no sneaking a look. You can fool yourself, but you can't fool a telepathic Talosian. Don't know who they are? Better have another read before taking the test.

Write your answers on paper. Humans may have 30 minutes to complete the test. Vulcans, Jedi Knights and Time Lords get 15 minutes. Ewoks may have three weeks.

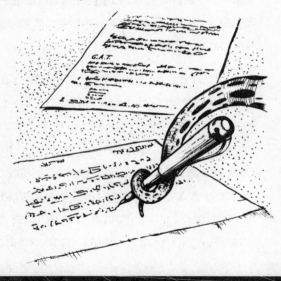

>>>

PROCEED . . .

THE QUESTIONS

1/ If your hosts said they had a Dewback ready for you, would they expect you to:
a/ Eat it
b/ Hunt it
c/ Wear it
d/ Ride it

2/ You are introduced to Hammerhead and so are probably:
a/ In trouble
b/ On the bridge of the *Enterprise*
c/ In Mos Eisley
d/ In a temple on Bajor
e/ On the tropical world of Ithor

3/ The Devil's Tower in Wyoming, USA, was used as a meeting place by:
a/ Humans working on the Stargate project
b/ The Coneheads
c/ Close Encounter aliens
d/ ET

4/ The tentacled being known as Cthulhu is:
a/ A type of Skrull
b/ An enemy of the Time Lords
c/ The leader of the Old Ones
d/ An ally of the evil Emperor Zurg
e/ The secret master of the Vulcan T'Pol

5/ Fire Balloons are:
a/ Dangerous inhabitants of the Trifid Nebula
b/ What happens after dinner if you eat too much
c/ Toys owned by Vulcan children
d/ An ancient Martian race
e/ The informal name for Klingon escape pods

6/ Returning home, you find that your bedroom is suddenly full of Goa'uld. Would you:
a/ Frown – it's a kind of radioactive space waste made by starship warp engines
b/ Smile – they're a form of money on Tatooine
c/ Run – they're a race of snake-like parasites
d/ Scream – they are a race of snake-like parasites and only the sound of a human voice can kill them

7/ You are lucky enough to be invited to a Minbari home for dinner. On no account should you show up with:
a/ Flowers that are already in bloom
b/ Shoes that are made of leather
c/ Your head uncovered
d/ Alcohol of any kind

8/ The being known as the Silver Surfer used to be in the employment of:
a/ Galactus
b/ The Skrull Empire
c/ Green Lantern Corps
d/ The Post Office

9/ On an exchange visit to Rigel IV you would expect to speak:

a/ English

b/ Rigelian

c/ Klingon

d/ Telepathically

10/ Match up each of these seven alien artefacts with the correct race that created them:

a/	Hand of Omega	1/	Centauri
b/	The Monolith	2/	Klingons
c/	Cosmic Cube	3/	Time Lords
d/	Gateway to Thirdspace	4/	Skrulls
e/	Sword of Kahless	5/	Unknown
f/	Guardian of Forever	6/	Vorlons
g/	The Eye	7/	Unknown

11/ Dana Scully's baby is called:

a/ Fox

b/ Walter

c/ Sally

d/ William

e/ Chris

12/ When receiving a dinner invitation from the Kanamit it is best to decline politely because:

a/ They are a race of dangerous shapeshifters

b/ They have no table manners

c/ They eat humans

d/ They have no after-dinner conversation

e/ There's always an argument about who sits where

13/ Arriving at your local space port you are told there is a Pak'ma'ra waiting for you. Do you:

a/ Eat it

b/ Ride it

c/ Flee in terror

d/ See who it is

14/ Match the following dangerous alien life forms with the planet on which they were first encountered:

a/	'Alien'	1/	Earth
b/	Predator	2/	Acheron
c/	Id Monster	3/	Mars
d/	Wampa Ice Creature	4/	Tatooine
e/	Chupacabra	5/	Cestus III
f/	Gorn	6/	Hoth
g/	Cyclopean	7/	Earth
h/	Sarlacc	8/	Altair-4

15/ At a party you overhear someone saying, "Understanding is a three-edged sword." The person speaking is probably a:

a/ Vulcan

b/ Romulan

c/ Vorlon

d/ Wormhole Alien

e/ Time Lord

16/ An ancient Martian spacecraft was dug up by which well-known investigator:

a/ Quatermass

b/ Ex-FBI Special Agent Mulder

c/ Budd Hopkins

d/ Lorne Mason

17/ You are giving a dinner party for ten friends from various planets. Which alien species should NOT be seated next to each other for fear of igniting old galactic conflicts over your carefully prepared main course?

a/	Dire Wraith	1/	Bajoran
b/	Sontaran	2/	Shadow
c/	Cardassian	3/	Skrull
d/	Vorlons	4/	Rutan
e/	Narn	5/	Centauri

18/ Finally, you are at another cosmic party (you lucky thing) and your host introduces you to a number of well-known faces. You need to make small talk and so it is vital that you remember their home worlds quickly. Match the individuals with their planet of origin or simply die of social embarrassment:

a/	T'Pol	1/	Alpha Centauri
b/	G'Kar	2/	Qo'noS
c/	Mork	3/	Bajor
d/	ALF	4/	Skaro
e/	Ashtar	5/	Krypton
f/	Davros	6/	Vulcan
g/	Worf	7/	Melmac
h/	Major Kira Neryls	8/	Mon Calamari
i/	Chewbacca	9/	Gallifrey
j/	The Master	10/	Duckworld
k/	Delenn	11/	Kashyyyk
l/	Clark Kent	12/	Minbar
m/	Howard the Duck	13/	Narn
n/	Admiral Ackbar	14/	Ork

THE ANSWERS

Score as following:

1/   a: 0 b: 0 c: 0 d: 10

2/   a: 0 b: 0 c: 10 d: 0 e: 15

3/   a: 0 b: 0 c: 5 d: 0

4/   a: 0 b: 0 c: 10 d: 0 e: 0

5/   a: 0 b: 0 c: 0 d: 10 e: 0

6/   a: 0 b: 0 c: 10 d: 0

7/   a: 0 b: 0 c: 0 d: 10

8/   a: 10 b: 0 c: 0 d: 0

9/   a: 10 b: 15 c: 0 d: 0

10/ Five points for each correct pairing:
    a: 3 b: 5 or 7 c: 4 d: 6 e: 2 f: 5 or 7 g: 1

11/ a: 0 b: 0 c: -5 d: 10 e: 0

12/ a: 0 b: 0 c: 15 d: 0 e: 0

13/ a: 0 b: 0 c: 0 d: 15

14/ Ten points for each correct pairing:
    a: 2 b: 1 or 7 c: 8 d: 6 e: 1 or 7 f: 5 g: 3 h: 4

15/ a: 0 b: 0 c: 15 d: 0 e: 0

16/ a: 15 b: 0 c: 0 d: 0

17/ Ten points for each correct pairing:
    a: 3 b: 4 c: 1 d: 2 e: 5

18/ Five points for each correct pairing:
    a: 6 b: 13 c: 14 d: 7 e: 1 f: 4 g: 2
    h: 3 i: 11 j: 9 k: 12 l: 5 m: 10 n: 8

DID YOU PASS?

There are a maximum of 400 points up for grabs.
Here's what your score means:

340 – 400

Excellent – Earth Diplomatic Corps could use you urgently. This is your chance to see the galaxy at the taxpayer's expense. Sign up now.

280 – 335

Good – You are more than ready to travel the interstellar highway. Good luck and watch out for the bad guys.

180 – 275

Fair – You just scraped a pass. Take care out there. Try not to cause any interplanetary wars, and remember if you do – you're own your own. Make sure you take this alien guide with you to fill in the blanks.

80 – 175

Poor – Read the guide again and this time put your brain back inside your head first.

0 – 75

There are lumps of rock on Norvall II that have scored higher than you.

FURTHER READING

Unfortunately, owing to the trade restrictions on imports into undeveloped worlds, none of the following works is currently available on Earth. However, once off-world, the space traveller should find them at any respectable bookshop or spaceport:

By the same author:
Gallifrey on Thirty Dollars a Day
Stairs? What Stairs? A Pocket Guide to Skaro

General:
Men are from Mars, Tentacled Drooling Things are from Venus by Razzox Fredom
101 Uses for a Dead Tribble by Chancellor Gorkon
Jabba the Hutt's Hip and Belly Diet by the Great One
Notes From a Very Small Planet by Mork.
Darth Vader: My Part in his Downfall by Wicket W Warrick
Captain Kirk's Mandolin and Other Stories by Mr Spock
Londo Mollari: His Life and Crimes by Ambassador G'Kar
My Way by Davros
Little Book of Pain by Garak of Cardassia

Readers trapped on the planet Earth who wish to establish contact with extraterrestrials are reminded of the SETI programme (see page 28). People anywhere can help with the SETI project by running a screensaver programme that downloads and analyses radio telescope data.

The SETI@home programme can be downloaded from the SETI websiter: www.setiathome.ssl.berkeley.edu/download.html. Like other screensavers, it activates when you leave your computer unattended. Then, while you are getting a fresh supply of chocolate biscuits, watching TV or sleeping, your computer will be helping the Search for Extraterrestrial Intelligence by analysing data specially captured by the world's largest radio telescope. If the computer you use isn't yours, check with the owner before downloading anything.

SPACE TRAVELLERS AND ABDUCTEES WHO ENCOUNTER
SPECIES NOT LISTED IN THIS EDITION OF THE
ALIEN ENCYCLOPEDIA ARE INVITED TO SEND THEIR
SUGGESTIONS TO:

> ANDREW DONKIN
> C/O HARPERCOLLINS PUBLISHERS LTD
> 77-85 FULHAM PALACE ROAD
> HAMMERSMITH
> LONDON W6 8JB
> ENGLAND
> EARTH

Andrew Donkin's early ambition was to be an astronaut. However, with the British space programme consisting of one washing-up bottle painted silver to look like a rocket, tragically it was not to be. Instead, he became a writer and is now the author of over 30 books for children, including the companion volume to this book, the *Weird Creatures Encyclopedia*. He has also written books for adults, television scripts and comics.

While researching this book he travelled extensively throughout the western spiral arm of the galaxy, including the notorious Trifid Nebula. You can find him and more cosmic material on the web at:
www.andrewdonkin.com

Paul Fisher-Johnson lives in crop-circle country in the west of England. As well as illustrating books, he is also a songwriter and performer.

INDEX

INDEX

WEIRD CREATURES ENCYLOPEDIA
The Ultimate A-Z

ANDREW DONKIN

Everything you need to know during a
field trip to Earth. Whether you're a visiting
alien or a resident human, this is your
essential survival guide...

DON'T LEAVE HOME
WITHOUT ONE...

Collins
VOYAGER

ISBN 0 00 713289 1

FIND